"You're a nice lady, Bev. You're a beautiful person."

Her pulse did a waltz up her arm, and the sensation irritated her. She didn't want to react to this man's attention—or any man's, for that matter.

"You're beautiful inside and out." Dale's gaze washed over her.

Bev didn't know what to say. She sensed he was sweet-talking her, and it was working. Her stomach had joined her pulse, and the two danced a jig through her until she felt unable to calm her emotions. She shook her head. "I try to be kind. Kindness looks beautiful."

"You're that, too." He reached for the carafe.

She watched him add coffee to his cup, then take a sip as if his mind had flown off somewhere else. Her emotions had been doing push-ups since Dale touched her arm.

Bev eyed her watch. "I suppose I'd better get home."

"I still have a favor to ask."

"Favor? I thought you'd asked it."

"I had two favors to ask."

Two? She noted an uncomfortable look edging across his face.

"This one is more personal," he said.

GAIL GAYMER MARTIN

is awed by God's blessings and amazed the Lord has led her to touch people's hearts and lives with her writing and speaking. Gail is a multipublished author of non-fiction and fiction for Steeple Hill and Barbour Publishing. Her novels have been finalists for numerous awards and have won the Holt Medallion (2001 and 2003), the Texas Winter Rose (2003) and the American Christian Romance Writers 2002 Book of the Year Award. Her Love Inspired novel, *A Love for Safekeeping,* was named *Romantic Times* Reviewers Choice Best Love Inspired Novel of 2002.

Besides writing, Gail travels across the country, guest speaking and presenting writing workshops. She lives in Lathrup Village, Michigan, with Bob—her husband and best friend. She loves to hear from her readers. Write to her at P.O. Box 760063, Lathrup Village, MI, 48076 and visit her Web site at www.gailmartin.com.

LOVING PROMISES

GAIL GAYMER MARTIN

Steeple
Hill®

Published by Steeple Hill Books™

STEEPLE HILL BOOKS

Steeple
Hill®

ISBN 0-373-87301-8

LOVING PROMISES

Copyright © 2005 by Gail Gaymer Martin

www.SteepleHill.com

Printed in U.S.A.

Let us hold unswervingly to the hope we profess, for he who promised is faithful. And let us consider how we may spur one another on toward love and good deeds.
—*Hebrews* 10:23–24

For my husband, Bob, whose loving ways have made me who I am today. You fill me with joy. Your support is unending, and your devotion is beyond description. Daily I thank the Lord for you.

Chapter One

"Where's your brother, Kristin?"

Kristin shrugged. "I don't know."

No surprise. Bev Miller bit back her irritation and shifted the shopping cart. She pulled bills from her wallet and paid the cashier. After the clerk dropped the last of the groceries into a plastic bag, Bev situated them into the basket, then moved away from the counter. Her mind raced with things she had left to do. Today was another hectic Saturday.

Bev craned her neck and spotted her seven-year-old son by the plastic toy display. "Michael, come here, please."

He didn't move. His gaze stayed riveted to a cardboard sheet with something intriguing attached.

"Michael!"

This time not only Michael but customers heard her raised voice. Embarrassed, Bev kept her eyes forward and rolled the basket toward the exit. Michael plodded behind her while Kristin pulled at the front of the cart, probably thinking she'd get home sooner if she sped them along.

When Michael reached Bev's side, his voice whined with disappointment. "Mom, I want a toy."

"Do you want to eat or have a new toy?" She wanted to swallow her words, knowing Michael preferred the junk in the plastic container. "Never mind. It's a moot point," she muttered.

"What's a mute point?" Michael's curious face tilted upward, awaiting Bev's response.

Bev's whole life seemed a moot point at times but never *mute*. She maneuvered through the doorway and held the children back before crossing the aisle to her car. "*Moot* not *mute*. It means it's debatable. There is no right or wrong answer."

"Then how come you always think you're right, Mom?" Michael asked in his I-didn't-get-my-way tone.

"When you're an adult, Michael, it will be your turn to be right."

He gave her a quizzical look and appeared to ponder the possibility.

"Grandma's coming tomorrow to live with us for a while, so we have lots to do, and everyone needs to cooperate."

"I can't wait to see Grandma," Kristin said, clapping her hands.

Bev knew why. Grandma spoiled the kids rotten.

A chill flew down her back from the damp Michigan weather, but also from thoughts of the coming event. Bev hadn't lived with her mother in many years, and she worried about two women under one roof. Could it work? Then again, being a single mom, Bev could use the support.

The mid-April wind forced them through the parking lot, and when she reached the car, Bev hit the remote, opened the trunk and loaded the groceries.

"Michael, would you push the basket over there, please?" Bev pointed toward the cart return across the aisle and a few spaces down.

He pulled his shoulder away from the car as if he were adhered to it. Then, apparently having a second thought, he perked up. He grasped the shopping basket handle and, making motor noises, took off like a race-car driver, zigzagging between the parked vehicles.

"Be careful," Bev called. She looked away long enough to open the car door so Kristin could climb inside. When she looked toward Michael, her heart thudded to a halt. Before she could yell, he'd performed a wheelie into a car backing into a slot.

Michael's face drained of color as the driver leaped from the sedan. In a heartbeat, Kristin jumped from the back seat and raced toward her brother. Bev darted after her, but the stranger stumbled over Kristin before she could pull her away.

"Why did you do that?" the man yelled. He faced a frightened-looking Michael.

"Move out of the way, kids," Bev said, her defenses rising. She peered at the trunk lid and saw no damage. "I'm sorry. Do you see any problem with your trunk?" She motioned to the car. "I don't."

He gazed at her with the bluest eyes she'd ever seen. "You should watch your kids."

"I said I'm sorry. And I do watch my children." She pulled them against her body with a protective arm.

"Maybe you should be more careful in a parking lot."

She sensed the stranger wanted to roll his eyes.

Instead, he bent over and surveyed the trunk lid, giving it a polish with the sleeve of his jacket. "Looks like he hit the bumper." He straightened his back and pointed his finger at Michael. "You could damage my car and hurt yourself with that silliness."

Bev felt her defense hackles rise as a facetious offer flew from her mouth. "Would you like my car insurance information just in case?" She assumed he'd say no since it was obvious the car had sustained no damage.

He tucked his fingers into his jeans pockets and rolled back on his heels. "No," he said, "but how about your driver's license?"

She drew up her shoulders and fumbled through her wallet for her license.

He pulled a pen out of his shirt pocket, then patted

the others as if looking for something. "I don't have any paper."

Bev reined in a smart remark and dug into her handbag. She grasped a scrap and handed it to him.

The man jotted down the information, slid it into his pocket, then handed back Bev's license before turning to Michael. "You'd better be more careful, young man. You could get hurt."

Michael took a step backward without responding.

Kristin, four going on forty, bustled toward the man, her fist planted on one hip. "You know what?"

The man's eyebrows shot upward.

Kristin didn't let his expression sway her. "Jesus says you should forgive others so God will forgive you."

His blue eyes widened, and Bev contained her amusement while the man stood speechless. As irritating as he was, she saw a spark of something she liked in his eyes that made him amazingly appealing.

Without further comment, she aimed the children toward her car and marched them back across the aisle in safety. When she looked in her rearview mirror, the good-looking stranger was still scrutinizing her.

Dale Levin hadn't been able to dismiss the vision of the woman from the grocery-store parking lot. She was feisty, he decided. Feisty and definitely pretty. Her unruly honey-colored hair looked sun-bleached and her attempt to keep it pinned back was about as useless as keeping her two rambunctious kids in tow. She should have left them home with their dad. He'd never have forgiven himself if the boy had been injured.

The little girl's comment rattled him. Though he guessed she was only a preschooler, she had tried to put him in his place. When she grew up, she would probably be as spirited as her mother. But the child's words didn't dent Dale's conviction. As far as he was concerned, God's promises seemed as empty as the shopping cart the boy had rammed into his bumper.

Dale pushed his foot against the brake and slowed for a stoplight. As always, his thoughts drifted to his parents and the reason for his visit home. Since his mother had been diagnosed with multiple sclerosis, his life hadn't been the same. Neither had his father's, and this weekend, his goal was to convince his dad he needed to get professional help for his mother's care. His father couldn't do it alone any longer. Dale wished he could spend more time at home, but he lived an hour away in Grand Rapids and his work was there.

His parents had always been strong Christians. They'd raised him the same way, but now, when he saw what his mother and father were going through, he'd taken a different slant on the Lord and definitely on marriage. His parents had the perfect marriage, he'd always thought—one he could never emulate.

So he'd resolved to avoid disillusionment by remaining single. It made sense to him. He'd been content the way he was and had no desire to deal with the sadness involved in falling in love. Life was something he couldn't count on. His father's pain as he watched his wife slip away—and his own sorrow—was almost more than Dale could bear.

The stoplight turned green and Dale stepped on the gas. His mind drifted once again to the parking-lot incident. Part of marriage was parenting, an experience he'd never know. He touched his shirt pocket and felt the scrap of paper inside. At the next stoplight, he withdrew it and scanned the information. Beverly Miller. He skimmed farther and saw she lived on Franklin Street, not too far from his parents. Irritated with himself, he folded the paper. Why did he care where she lived?

As he started to slip the scrap into his pocket, something caught his eye. He unfolded the sheet and saw a section from a church bulletin—Fellowship Church where his father attended. On the back, a child had drawn a picture.

He studied the simple line sketch of a bungalow surrounded by flowers, smoke curling from the chimney and sunshine streaking the sky. Standing on a sidewalk were a woman and two children—stick figures but he got the message and realized he'd probably been wrong about leaving the kids home with her husband. It appeared she was a single mom.

Two kids. Dale had been an only child. He'd grown up alone, and he'd been his parents' total focus. They'd done everything for him, and now he would do everything he could for them. He wished the Lord felt the same way.

The traffic moved ahead again, and finally Dale pulled into his parents' driveway. Propping the groceries against the doorjamb, Dale turned the knob and stepped into the back hallway. He plopped the packages onto the counter, then strode down the hallway to his parents' bedroom.

He stood in the doorway to see if his mother was sleeping. Every time he saw her this way, his heart broke once more. As he turned to go, he heard her say his name. Her speech had been one attribute not highly affected by the disease.

"Hi, Mom," he said, stepping closer. "Do you want me to raise the shades?"

"Only a little," she said. "The light hurts my eyes until I adjust."

He crossed the room and lifted the shade a few inches. Sunlight seeped onto the carpet. He moved to her bedside and lifted her head a little, propping a couple of pillows beneath her neck to raise her. "Comfortable?"

"Comfortable and happy when you're here."

He sat on the edge of the mattress and drew her hand into his. "Dad should be here soon to help you dress."

Her eyelids lowered. "I hate your father having to leave work to dress me. I only wish…" Her words faded away.

"I have groceries to put away," he said, releasing her

hand and rising. He needed to get away from the pain he saw in his mother's eyes. Dale recalled years earlier when she'd been a vibrant woman, before the disease had disabled her. Science didn't have an answer for MS. No one did except God, and He was keeping quiet.

He left the room, wishing he had a sibling. He mulled over the idea of someone sharing his concern for his parents. Someone to talk with now when he felt so stressed.

In the kitchen, he began storing the groceries. Before he finished, the back door opened and his father stepped inside, carrying a fast-food bag. "You went grocery shopping," Al Levin said, setting down the sack. "Thanks."

"Just a few things, but I see you picked up something."

His father leaned against the kitchen counter and tilted his head toward the sack. "It's a milk shake. Your mom loves ice cream so I bring her a treat once in a while." He grabbed the fast-food bag. "I'll take it to her."

Dale finished storing the groceries and pulled out a package of meat for dinner. He'd wrestled with himself all afternoon about talking to his father about the situation with his mom. He vowed to himself he'd do it this weekend. No time seemed right.

When his father returned, his eyes were misted. They seemed to be so often, and the emotion affirmed Dale's earlier thoughts. Being single was easier.

Al moved to the kitchen counter and opened a canister. "Coffee?" he asked, spooning grounds into the coffeemaker.

"Sounds good." Dale wiped off the counter and draped the dishcloth over the sink. He rested against the counter and organized his thoughts while the coffee brewed. Seeing his dad's weary eyes and the stress on his face made the task disheartening.

Dale set two mugs on the table as his fortitude kicked into high gear. Before he settled onto a kitchen chair, he drew up his shoulders, ready for the argument.

His father brought over the pot and poured them each a cup, then returned the coffee to the warmer. He ambled back with a plate of cookies from the counter and set them on the table. "Annie Dewitt gave me a tin of homemade cookies at the pharmacy yesterday."

Dale picked up a cookie and took a bite.

"I probably told her once how your mom used to make me oatmeal cookies."

Hearing the reference to his mother, Dale held the cookie suspended, then lowered it while his mouth worked around the words that had to be spoken. "Dad, you know Mom's getting worse."

"She's as good as can be expected," his father said, lifting the cup and taking a sip of the black coffee.

"I think caring for her alone is too much for you."

"No problem is too much with the Lord, Dale."

Dale ran his finger around the rim of the mug, realizing his father wasn't making the talk easy. He felt his ʰirit sink as he struggled for the right words. "I worry ᵗwo of you."

"I know you do, but we're fine. Your mom and I have shared so many joys along the way they far outweigh the sorrows," he added. "God's been good to us."

His father's words knocked the wind out of him. Dale's arguments fell into dust. How could he tell his father that God hadn't been good to them? Tomorrow. Maybe when his father got home from church, he could pursue the topic. Dale shoved the debate into the back of his mind and took a drink of coffee.

Silence hung over them until his father rose and set his cup in the sink. When he turned, Dale saw the beginnings of a mission etched on his face. "I was hoping you'd go to church with me tomorrow."

Dale faltered. "Church?" Beverly Miller's church, he recalled. He hadn't gone in a long time, even when his father asked. "I thought I'd stay home and keep an eye on Mom while you go."

"I miss your mom beside me. Just thought it would be nice to have my son there for a change."

Sadness washed over Dale. "Okay, Dad. I'll go with you." Yet his thoughts had already begun to formulate tomorrow's battle. He had to make his dad listen to reason.

Bev guided the children into their Sunday-school rooms. She liked to attend the service that offered worship and Sunday school at the same time. When she took the kids to worship, her own attention was sacrificed.

Today she needed to focus on the pastor's message. She needed time for prayer and meditation—not time to referee her children's arguments.

Her mother's expected arrival filled her with trepidation, and Bev would do anything to avoid stress between herself and her mother.

She found a pew near the back, opened the bulletin and scanned it. The singles' events caught her eye. She had never felt as if she were single. Yet her thoughts shifted to the man with the amazing eyes she'd met in the grocery-store parking lot the day before.

The organ music began, and her thoughts faded. The song of praise flowed into the rafters as the worshippers' voices rose with joy. Bev listened to the lessons, waiting for something to soothe her fears and hoping God had some special words to touch her heart.

Nothing struck her as the pastor's lessons closed. She bowed her head, asking God to let her heart calm and her faith be strong.

"I'll leave you with these words from Philippians, the fourth chapter," Pastor Brian said as the service closed. "Think about the message during the week and let it lie on your heart."

Let it lie on your heart. Bev's head lifted and her pulse tripped.

"'Do not be anxious about anything, but in everything, by prayer and petition, with thanksgiving, present your requests to God. And the peace of God, which transcends all understanding, will guard your hearts and your minds in Christ Jesus.'" The pastor closed the Bible and stepped away.

The choir rose, and Bev sat, her mouth gaping at the simple message that meant so much to her. God had heard her prayer and had sent her something to lie on her heart. *With thanksgiving present your requests to God.* Despite all her problems—the loss of her mate, the struggle to raise her young children, the loneliness she'd felt for an intimate love—God had kept her and her children safe and in His care.

The choir's praise wrapped around her heart. If she and her mother had conflicts, she would turn to the Lord in grateful prayer. She was never alone with Jesus by her side.

A calm swept over her, and when the service ended, her steps felt lighter as she moved into the aisle. Before Bev had made any progress working her way through the worshippers, she spotted her friend from the child-care facility where she worked.

"Annie," Bev said, looking at the beautiful toddler in her arms. "Hi, Gracelynne. Every day she seems to grow more. Like a weed."

"A heavy weed," Annie said, shifting the child's weight. "Ken had a rush job today, or he'd be doing the toting."

Bev brushed the toddler's soft cheek. When she lifted her gaze, her stomach somersaulted. Al Levin, her pharmacist, was standing with the stranger who'd been filling her thoughts. "Who is that?" she asked Annie, giving a nod in their direction.

Annie glanced over her shoulder. "That's Mr. Levin's son, I think. He comes into town to visit his mother. She has MS."

Bev's heart sank. She'd been rude to the man when he'd probably been preoccupied with more serious concerns. Before she could look away, their eyes met.

The last thing Bev wanted to do was face Mr. Levin's son. She took a step backward to make her escape, but Annie's question stopped her.

"Where's your mom? I thought she'd be here."

Bev dragged her mind from her predicament. "She's arriving this evening. The kids are so anxious." She shifted farther away. "And speaking of them, I'd better go—" She stopped in midsentence, cornered.

"Annie," Al Levin said. "I want you to meet my son, Dale."

Annie hoisted Gracelynne higher on her hip, and Dale offered a handshake.

"You're the cookie lady," Dale said.

Annie's eyebrows lifted, and Bev wondered what that meant.

Al chuckled and explained the story, then focused on Bev. "I know we've met at the pharmacy, but—"

"Bev Miller. You've filled lots of prescriptions for

us." She forced herself to look at Dale. "I've already met your son. Sort of."

Her "sort of" caught everyone's attention, and she quickly explained their parking-lot accident.

As her story ended, Gracelynne began to fidget while Annie tried to soothe her with no success. "I'd better get her home. It's nap time." She gave a warm smile to Dale. "Nice to meet you."

Al gave Dale's arm a pat. "Hang on, would you? I need to talk to someone for just a minute."

He sped away, leaving Bev and Dale facing each other alone.

Chapter Two

Bev gaped at Dale, then words exited their mouths like one litany. "I'm sorry about—" They laughed as the amusing coincidence broke the tension.

"We were both upset," Bev said. "I realized after we left that you were worried more about Michael than your car."

Dale flexed his palm. "Nothing more needs to be said. We were both edgy."

Though the issue had been settled in Dale's mind, she had more to say.

"Your son's name is Michael," he said, more than asked.

She nodded.

"Typical boy."

"You probably know. I'm sure you did the same things when you were a kid."

"But I never got caught."

There you go, Bev thought, so you're not perfect. She fiddled with her shoulder bag. She'd never known a man to look so searchingly into her eyes.

With his gaze capturing hers, he reached toward his pocket. "By the way, this is yours." He pulled out a wad of paper.

As soon as it hit her hand, she recognized it. "Why are you return—"

"I noticed a picture on the back. I suppose a drawing by one of your children. I figured you'd want it back since you'd hung on to it."

Bev remembered shoving the bulletin into her handbag. "Kristin, my four-year-old, sketched it." She unfolded the sheet and glanced at the drawing. "It's us. Our house and family."

"A nice one from the looks of it."

She eyed the bright colors and grinned. "I suppose."

"Flowers, smoke curling from the chimney, all signs of a child who's happy and content," he said. "Sometimes kids see life differently than adults do."

She wondered what he meant by that statement.

Sadness filled his eyes, adding to her curiosity.

She held up the paper. "Thanks for returning this." She slid it into her shoulder bag and gave it a pat. "I'd better find my kids before one of them starts doing wheelies in the church parking lot."

"See you around." He tucked his hands into his pants pockets.

"Could be," she said as her mind clung to his comment about kids seeing life differently.

Dale dragged the rake through the soggy leaves left behind by winter. A spring chill hung in the air, but the sun made an appearance from behind a cloud and sent the promise of warmer days.

The weekend had brought about the unexpected, and it had nothing to do with weather. He thought of Bev Miller and her brood. He'd wondered if he would see her at the service. She was an interesting woman and, like a mother hen, so defensive of her chicks.

Dale chuckled to himself. Thinking of chicks, Bev was definitely one. He envisioned her slender form and youthful appearance, almost too young-looking to be a mother. Though Dale dated occasionally, he would never get serious with a woman—especially one with kids. Dating might pass the long evenings in Loving after his mom went to sleep and his father settled in front of the TV. But he couldn't date a woman with a family. She needed far more than he could give, and Bev Miller had a doozy of a family.

He couldn't understand why she remained in his thoughts, except he admired her spunky spirit, her devotion to her family and her smile. He could only guess she provided a distraction from his melancholy feelings.

Dale's mind shifted to his parents inside the house.

The pharmacy was closed on Sunday, and Dale hoped his dad could get some rest today.

His rake caught on a tree root, and Dale loosened the snag, then added more dried foliage to the pile. He had to leave for home shortly, and he faced the moment. He either had to talk with his father now or break the promise he'd made to himself. Dale didn't like either choice.

Hearing the back door close, Dale turned and saw his dad heading across the spongy lawn. "Thanks, but I know you have to get going soon." He gestured toward the pile. "Just leave that. I can use it for compost."

Agreeing, Dale dragged the debris to the back corner of the yard, then propped the rake beside the back stoop. His father followed him up the stairs and into the back hallway.

Dale took off his shoes and set them on a mat. His father did the same, and, stocking-clad, they walked into the kitchen. "How about some coffee before you leave?"

"No, thanks," Dale said, pulling out a chair and sitting at the kitchen table, "but I do think we need to talk about Mom."

His father's head snapped upward, and a wary look settled on his face. "What about Mom? I thought we talked about this yesterday."

"We did, but I didn't say all I needed to say. Can you sit for a minute?"

Al moved toward the table as if he'd rather do anything else in the world. When he reached it, he turned

the chair sideways and sat. He clasped his hands together, his elbows draped on his knees, and stared at the
floor. "I love your mother with all my heart, and I wish
I could make things different for her."

"But you can't, Dad." Dale wanted so badly to ask
the Lord for help, but he fought the urge. Why give in
to a God who promised compassion, then showed none?
"Dad, you're killing yourself. Working all day at the
pharmacy while running back and forth to meet Mom's
needs is doing you in. The doctor told you the same
thing. You can't keep this up without getting some help."

Al swiveled on the chair and stared at the tabletop a
moment before facing him. "I have help, Son. The Lord
is my strength. I read the Bible every night, and God is
with me. I made a promise many years ago to stick by
your mother in sickness and in—"

"Dad, I'm not suggesting you don't stick by Mom.
I'm suggesting you get help."

Al pulled his shoulders back and riveted his gaze to
Dale's. "I'm not putting your mother in a home."

"You don't have to. Let's find someone to come in
and help out. A caregiver. You could find someone in
Loving to come in a few hours a day."

His father's determined expression didn't waver. "I
can't ask your mother to let a stranger dress her."

Another thought came to Dale's mind. "Could you
hire someone to fill in at the pharmacy and you stay
home with Mom, or maybe work part-time for a while?"

His father gave him a blank stare. "I can't do that now, Dale. One day, but not now."

Dale grasped his father's knotted hands, longing to make him listen. "Please, then just think about hiring someone. If you believe God is listening, ask him to help you find the right person."

Al shifted his gaze and shook his head. "You disappoint me, Son. You were raised in the faith. Why don't you know that the Lord is filled with compassion and mercy?"

Dale's chest tightened and he lifted his hand as he pointed a quaking finger toward the doorway. "Do you see any mercy in that bedroom, Dad?"

His father's eyes widened, but he didn't respond.

"I'm sorry. I'm truly sorry…but I don't see one particle of mercy in that room at all."

Friday evening, Bev aimed the shopping cart down the canned-goods aisle. Since her mother's arrival, Bev had had a reprieve from cooking. Her mother had taken over, and although they'd had a few stressful moments when it came to disciplining the kids, sharing her home hadn't been too bad.

Besides being preoccupied with her mother's arrival, Bev couldn't help thinking of Dale. Seeing him at the worship service validated her finding. Dale had been more concerned about Michael than his car. She'd wanted to tell him her feelings at church, but he'd stopped her.

She still couldn't wipe the cart incident from her thoughts. If a car had been speeding through the parking lot that day, Michael might have been injured. Speeding. Even speeding with a grocery cart caused her heart to stand still. Since her husband's death, every time Bev saw a motorcycle tear down the highway, anger flamed inside her. Anger and sadness.

Jesse had tried to be a good husband and father. He spent time with the kids and paid the bills, but his love of speed and excitement had ended his life too soon. She wished he'd been half as concerned about racing as Dale Levin, who'd cautioned Michael to be careful. Jesse hadn't listened any better than their son. But she had loved him when they'd married, and she missed many things about him, despite their problems.

Still, life went on. Bev kept her two lively children dressed and well-fed. And loved. That's what counted. Being on her own had its faults, but no more than being in a stressful relationship.

Bev glanced at her list, eyed the shelves and selected a couple of cans of corn, then headed for the green beans.

"Hello."

Her hand faltered, and she turned toward the voice. Her pulse skittered when she saw his face. "Dale. What are you doing here?"

"Same as you." He grinned and gestured to the basket. "I'm shopping for my folks. We're having company tomorrow, my dad tells me."

She waited, thinking he'd say something else, but he didn't. Finally she said it. "Guess who's coming to dinner?"

He'd caught the movie title, she noticed from his grin. Yet a puzzled look settled on his face.

"An old high-school friend," he said.

"Mildred Browne."

His eyebrows lifted. "How do you know that? Dad called her Millie."

She enjoyed having the upper hand. "She's my mother."

"You're kidding." He shifted his cart to the side and rested his elbow against the handle. "How long will she be here?"

Bev ran her hand over her hair, sensing he was staring at it. "She decided to move back to town. My dad died a few years ago and she had nothing to hold her back from coming home. She grew up here."

"She's living with you?"

His gaze washed over her, and she suddenly felt uneasy. "Temporarily. She'll get her own place. Right now, Mom's goal is to renew old acquaintances and enjoy retirement. She's only fifty-nine."

"Wise goal." He rocked his cart back and forth. "I suppose I'll meet her tomorrow."

He looked over his shoulder as if ready to make his escape. Instead, he surprised her.

"Do you have time for a coffee?" he asked.

She glanced in the direction he'd looked and spotted

the superstore's small snack bar. Curious about why he'd asked, she studied him a moment before making her decision.

A serious look settled in his eyes, and she sensed he needed to talk. "I have a few minutes. Mom's with the kids."

"Great. It's better than standing here blocking the aisle." He flagged her forward and she led the way.

Bev sat while Dale paid for the coffees and brought them to the table. She took a sip of the frothy drink and licked the flavor from her lips. "Thanks," she said, her curiosity rising with each moment.

He didn't speak but sipped the drink, then pushed the cup in circles with his index finger.

"Funny how our folks know each other," she said finally to break the silence.

"It is." He didn't lift his eyes. "Since we got off on such a bad start, I was hoping we could smooth things out a little."

"Like you said, no problem." Just don't discipline my kids, she said to herself.

"Now that we've talked about our folks, what should I know about you?"

Nothing, she thought, then her feelings softened. The poor guy was trying to make amends like a Christian should. "I'm a widow with two children. That part you figured out."

"I didn't know you were a widow."

She shrugged, realizing he didn't know her well enough to understand that divorce was not part of her vocabulary. "I work at Loving Care. It's a child-care facility and handy because I can take Kristin along. She starts school in September."

He nodded, then looked thoughtful as if he wanted to know more, but she wasn't ready to tell him.

"How about you?" she asked.

"I live in Grand Rapids and work for a business firm there. Not much to tell. I've never married. I'm an only child."

"That explains it," Bev said, before she could slap her mouth closed.

"Explains what?"

"Why you don't like kids."

"It's nothing to do with liking. I'm not used to being around kids."

"You'll have a chance tomorrow."

He looked surprised, and it pleased her to see him out of control.

"Didn't you know your dad invited all of us?"

"No."

"Mom tried to convince him the kids would be too much for your mother, but he said she'd love it." She let her gaze linger on his face, wondering if he were upset.

"You mean you *and* your kids are coming?"

His response answered her question. "Sorry, it wasn't my decision."

It was his turn to look uneasy for a change. "I didn't mean it that way."

She wondered what way he did mean it. Obviously, the man didn't like children. Too bad, she thought, because they were invited and they would be there.

Bev parked in front of the neat ranch house, trying to calm herself. "I hope these people know what they're in for."

Mildred looked into the back seat and gave the kids a smile. "Al said they'd be a godsend. I'm not debating Al or the Lord."

Bev chuckled at her mother's comment, then turned and gave the children her final lecture followed by their resounding groan from the back seat. When she finished, she thought of her mother's comment and the pastor's Sunday lesson. *Do not be anxious about anything, but in everything, by prayer and petition, with thanksgiving present your requests to God.* Bev needed some bended-knee time with the Lord.

When she unlocked the door, the children unhooked their seat belts and tumbled from the car. Bev grabbed her dinner contribution and said a short prayer as she headed for the door. Between dealing with her kids and knowing Dale would be there, she had a case of jitters.

"Welcome," Al said, as he greeted them. He gave Mildred a friendly hug and shook Bev's hand.

"Thanks for inviting us, Mr. Levin," Bev said as she ushered the children inside.

"Al, please. No need for formalities."

Mildred and the kids moved ahead to the living room, and Bev followed Al's direction by heading toward the kitchen with her dinner offerings.

A delectable aroma greeted her in the dining room and as she passed, she noticed the table was already set. At the doorway, she faltered. Dale stood beside the stove, stirring something with a large spoon. He looked amazing in a slate-blue crewneck sweater that hugged his broad chest. The sensation she experienced frightened her. "Hi," she said, forcing herself into the room.

Dale jumped and swung around as a glob of sauce fell to the floor. A grin made its way to his mouth. "You scared me."

"I noticed." She set the box on the counter and pulled off a sheet of paper towel to wipe up the mess.

He grasped her hand. "Let me do that," he said, taking the toweling.

The warmth of his fingers rolled up her arm.

He knelt and swiped at the spot, then rose.

His grin swept over her. "What's in the box?" he asked.

"A seven-layer salad and a key lime pie. Low-calorie, but don't tell anyone."

He looked inside the carton before his gaze drifted across her frame. "Why are you worried about calories?"

Bev felt a flush creeping up her neck. Too rattled to respond, she only chuckled.

Dale turned back to the box and slid the food into the refrigerator.

Bev watched him, thinking she'd be smart to leave the kitchen, but she didn't.

"What can I do to help?" she asked. Drawn by the aroma coming from the kettle and the desire to be in Dale's company, she made her way toward the stove to take a peek. "Stroganoff?"

He nodded. "Dad loves it, and the sauce is tasty and soft enough for my mom. She has a difficult time eating."

She didn't know how to respond to that so she looked around the kitchen for something to do. "I noticed the table is set. Give me another job."

"Just sit there and look pretty." He tilted his head toward the kitchen table.

His comment addled her. "I meant something easier than that." Amazed at her rising emotions, she lifted the lid on a smaller pan. Noodles. Nothing she could do with that.

Heat raced through her body, and she stepped back from the stove, but the warmth persisted. Her discomfort grew. She knew they were flirting with each other, but she'd become too inexperienced to handle it. Two children and a few years without a man's attention made her a novice when it came to being coy with Dale.

She moved closer to the doorway. "If you don't need me, I'll go save the others from my kids."

A light flashed in Dale's head. He needed someone, and maybe Bev could help. He pivoted toward her. "You could do one thing."

"Great. Name it."

"Give me some ideas."

"About the stroganoff?"

"I need some help with—" he lowered his voice "—my mom."

"Your mother?" She gave him a puzzled look and stepped closer. Was he asking her to give up her job at Loving Care? "What kind of help?"

"You've lived in Loving a long time. I wondered if you know anyone who could come in weekdays and help with my mother. My dad's killing himself, and he won't even consider getting help."

"Why not?" Her expression reflected her empathy.

"He has every excuse in the book, including he has the Lord and he needs nothing else."

"There's truth to that, Dale."

"Don't you start," he said, hearing his voice snap.

She veered back as if he'd struck her.

"I'm sorry. That's a sensitive issue for me." For some reason he wanted to explain, but he clamped his mouth closed. First she wouldn't care about his issues, and second, he didn't talk about his feelings. Emotions didn't count. Reality did.

She didn't say anything for a moment, but from the flush in her cheeks, he knew he'd upset her.

"I know child-care workers," she said finally, her voice calm and businesslike, "but I really don't have contact with people who do adult care."

"How about at church?"

Her frown softened as she looked at him. "I'll think about it. Next time I'm there, I'll look around and see if anyone comes to mind. I can't promise you anything."

"I realize that. Just let me know if you think of anyone. I'd appreciate it."

He was touched by her concerned look, and his rude behavior poked at him. "I didn't mean to sound so abrupt earlier. You hit a sore issue with me, and I spoke before I thought."

"You do that a lot," she said, but her voice was soft rather than fiery. He sensed she meant it as a kind criticism rather than a smart remark.

"I'll have to work on that," he said. Without thinking he reached up and brushed a strand of hair from her cheek.

Her eyes widened, and without a further comment, she hurried out of the room.

Dale watched her vanish and wondered what had gotten into him. He'd called her pretty, snapped at her and now fondled her cheek. He'd become a paradox of behavior.

Why was he toying with a woman who had children? His conduct was not only foolhardy, it could be hurtful. He had no intention of tangling his life around a ready-made family. He had enough to worry about.

Dale adjusted the heat on the burners, then pulled a small plate from the cabinet and sneaked out a spoonful of noodles, added some stroganoff sauce, then grabbed a fork and used the hallway door to his mother's bedroom.

"Hungry?" he asked as he stepped inside.

"A little. I hear voices. Is the company here?"

Dale nodded. "Dad thought you should rest until after dinner. Then you'll feel more like visiting."

She managed a faint smile. "We both agreed that was best."

He adjusted her pillows, then covered her with a napkin and spoon-fed her some of the mixture.

"That's plenty," Dotty said after a few mouthfuls. "I'll just rest here until everyone's finished eating. Now go and have a nice time."

Her brave acceptance of her disease twisted through Dale's senses. He kissed his mother's cheek and returned to the kitchen.

In a few minutes, he announced dinner, and he watched Michael cringe when their eyes met. He felt guilty and figured he should be adult enough to say something to relieve the kid's panic. He forced a grin. "You haven't been running any more cars off the road have you, Michael?"

The boy looked at him with wary eyes until he realized Dale was teasing. Finally he grinned. "I'm more careful now."

"That's good," he said, figuring he'd done his duty.

When they'd all assembled around the table, his father asked them to join hands, and, after the blessing and a special thanks for their guests, the meal began. The conversation was genial and relaxed until Kristin spilled her glass of milk.

"Kristin," Bev said, "you have to learn to be careful. You do this all the time."

Dale leaped from the table to grab a roll of paper towel as he winced at the "all the time" line. He blotted the mess while Bev did her best to help. When he returned to his seat, he avoided the soggy cloth as best he could, grasping his patience.

Things settled down again, and Dale's attention shifted between Bev and his father's friendship with Millie. He'd never seen his father with a female friend, and it troubled him.

"It's great to have you all here," Al said, "and Millie, you look really good. Just like old times."

"Forty years plus."

"Has it been that long? I can't tell you how many times I've told Dotty about some of our shenanigans. She loves to hear me talk about them."

Bev's mother grinned. "I bet I remember a few escapades you've forgotten."

He reached across the table to pat her hand. "I bet you do."

Shenanigans? Escapades? Dale wanted to ask what

they meant. He couldn't imagine his father with another woman except his mother. The familiarity didn't set well with Dale. While his mother was in the bedroom alone, his father was sharing memories with another woman.

Dale fought the tension that knotted inside him. When the meal ended, he brought out dessert, grateful that the children had settled for store-bought cookies and had gone into the living room to play. Dale had dragged out a huge box of his boyhood Tinkertoys from his parents' storage closet. Today he saw their wisdom in insisting they hang on to them. What damage could a child do with those?

Moments later his question was answered by the sound of glass shattering.

Chapter Three

Bev jumped up before he did, and they darted into the living room together, their arms brushing as they passed through the doorway. The softness of the simple touch rippled down his arm, but when he entered the living room, the memory faded. Michael stood above a broken candy dish, part of it on the table and shards on the floor.

"What did you do?" Bev asked.

"Nothing," Michael said.

Dale struggled against voicing his irritation. Dishes didn't just jump into the air and break.

"You obviously did something," Bev said.

Dale noticed the wooden toy configuration in the boy's hand. An airplane, he figured. "Were you flying your plane?" He gave Michael one of his steady stares.

The boy nodded his head. "It's a space missile," he muttered.

Dale took the creation from the boy's hands and pulled apart the pieces. "Now, it's nothing." How could anyone deal with the constant distraction of having a houseful of kids?

As he dropped the pieces on the floor and turned to get something to gather the glass, he noticed Bev's look, then the boy's, but he plowed ahead. "I only hope this isn't something precious to my mother."

As the words left his mouth, his father came into the room with a mini-vacuum. He eyed the situation and smiled. "Glass candy dish. Nothing that can't be replaced." He approached the children. "I hope neither of you cut yourself."

The children looked at their fingers, then shook their heads.

"Good." He lifted his gaze to Dale. "I'll clean this up. Why don't you two go back in and enjoy your dessert. When I'm through here, I'll bring in your mother. She's anxious to meet everyone."

Dale turned, catching a deeper scowl on Bev's face. He'd done it again. He seemed to be the bad guy, while his father had handled the situation with the kids perfectly.

When he and Bev returned to the dining room, the conversation seemed to lull. Dale figured Bev was annoyed with him, and Mildred was wondering what had happened.

Bev sat in her chair, her back stiff while Dale admitted to himself he didn't have a knack with kids. It was good he had no plans for fatherhood.

They sat in silence, waiting, and when his father returned, all eyes turned toward Dotty. Though frail, she was a pretty woman. She sat in a wheelchair, her gray hair combed in a simple style, her thin frame covered by a rose-colored outfit. Dale couldn't bear to see the change in her. When he shifted his focus, he saw the sadness he felt reflected in Bev's eyes.

"Hello," Dotty said, looking at Mildred. "I'm so pleased to meet you. Al has told me so many stories about you two." She shifted her focus. "And you must be Beverly."

"Bev, please, and I'm the mother of the two making noise in your living room. I'm sorry they broke one of your candy dishes."

"They're a dime a dozen. Did they find something to play with?"

"My old Tinkertoys," Dale said. "I always thought it was stupid to keep those things."

Al gestured toward Dale. "We've been keeping them for our grandchildren, but that seems unlikely."

Dale's pulse jolted from his father's unexpected admission. He clamped his jaw when he saw Bev's smirk.

"Tell me the best story about Al that comes to mind," Dotty said.

Mildred thought a minute before telling one of her favorites. Their laughter drew the children into the room, and Dale couldn't help but grin at them, quiet for a change and engrossed in the story of their grandmother's escapades.

The stories continued until Al suggested they move to the living room. "It's much more comfortable in there," Al said.

Dale checked his watch, amazed to see the amount of time they'd spent around the table.

"We should be going," Mildred said. "I'm sure Dotty's tired, and we all have church tomorrow."

When Dale saw Bev rise, carrying dishes into the kitchen, he followed. He stood beside her, and when she turned, they were so close a flowery scent enveloped him and he couldn't move. "You smell amazing," he said, noticing an uneasy look spread across Bev's face.

He wanted to step away, but his legs felt immobile so close to hers. Finally he found his voice, and his words broke the spell. "I'm sorry about the incident with the kids. I guess you're right."

"I am," she said. "Kids are part of the world. They make mistakes like we all do. Forgiveness is a gift God gives us. We can learn from that."

He nodded, not knowing what else to say, then took a step back. "Thanks for coming. This evening was wonderful for my mom. I haven't seen her have so much fun in a long time."

"It was a nice evening for all of us." She gave him a

nervous smile. "I got to know a side of my mother I've never seen before."

The tension subsided, replaced by an alien sensation that fluttered through him. Bev was a blend of good things, and he liked what he saw. Even defending her kids seemed right. He was tempting himself to possibilities he couldn't...wouldn't keep.

They stood a moment as if perplexed about what to do next. He searched her eyes, wondering if she sensed the same feelings. When she lowered her gaze, Dale touched her arm and steered her toward the dining room, stirred by a longing that addled him.

When he came through the doorway, Mildred stood and kissed his mother's cheek. "Thank you so much for having us."

"I hope we do this again," Dotty said.

Dale knew his mother was sincere, but his heart twisted as he noted the exhaustion in her face.

"Al tells me you just retired," Dotty said.

"Yes, from nursing," Mildred said.

A look flashed between Dale and his father. Had his father realized what that could mean? If Dale believed that God cared about them, he would think the Lord had really worked a miracle. Bev, also, sidled a questioning look at Dale. She lifted her eyebrows as if she were contemplating the same thoughts.

Dale leaned closer to her. "Do you think it's possible?"

"Hard to tell," she said, "but maybe."

The same warm feeling spread over him until the cold wind of reality struck him. Bev was wheedling her way into his thoughts and feelings. Attraction led to commitment, and commitment led to marriage, then family. He wanted none of either.

Bev shifted on the park bench, wishing it were padded, then grinned at her silly thought. The Saturday afternoon gifted her with a warm sun, and only an occasional chilly breeze ruffled her hair and sprinkled gooseflesh on her arms. Spring had truly arrived.

"Be careful, Michael," she called, as he released a swing that narrowly missed hitting Kristin's back.

Michael glanced Bev's way and went on about his play without batting an eye. Sometimes she thought he needed his hearing checked, but that was an excuse. He heard her. He just ignored her requests.

Bev shifted her gaze across new grass toward the fountain, and her pulse skipped. A man pushing someone in a wheelchair came into view, and she had no doubt who they were. Dale and Dotty. She angled away from them, not to avoid them exactly, but to give her time for thought.

For some reason, she sensed she and Dale were being thrust together. Coincidence seemed too simple. Michael ran into Dale's car, Dale's father and her mother were best friends, no matter where she went— church, grocery shopping or the park, Dale suddenly appeared. She lifted her eyes to heaven. *Lord, is this Your doing? And if so, what's the purpose?*

A thought washed over her. Maybe God had brought the two families together because Dotty needed care and Bev's mother was a caregiver. Was that the reason? With the possibility making sense, Bev relaxed. The thought had crossed her mind at dinner the week before. She sensed the same idea had struck Dale.

When Bev glanced again, she saw Dale and Dotty heading her way. She rose and gave them a wave, noting Dale's grin.

"Dale spotted you," Dotty said.

Bev leaned down and gave his mother a hug. "It's nice to see you."

"How about me?" Dale asked.

A moment passed before Bev realized what he meant, but before she could find something to say, Kristin's scream shattered the air. Bev spun toward the sound.

The child ran toward her, tears flowing from her eyes while her hand clutched her forehead.

"What happened?" Bev asked, pulling away her fingers. A dark welt rose below the little girl's hairline, a bruise already forming.

Dale stepped closer and pushed the girl's hair aside. "It's not bleeding, but she's going to have a knot there."

"What happened?" Bev asked again.

"Michael hit me with the swing," Kristin said between hiccoughing sobs.

Bev eyed the boy sitting on the swing seat and moving it in circles. He ignored the group huddled around Kristin. When he'd tightened the swing's chain, he lifted his feet and spun around until the momentum halted.

"Michael," she called. "Come here." She beckoned at him, but he only began winding the chains again for another spinning ride.

"Michael!" Dale bellowed.

Bev's heart lurched at his yell while anger shot through her, but she glanced at Dotty and held her tongue.

Michael unwound like a loosened coil of rope and approached them with his head hanging.

"I want to talk with you later," Bev hissed to Dale. Gritting her teeth, she turned her attention to Michael.

"What did you do to Kristin?"

"Noth—" He lifted his eyes to Dale and changed his tack. "I didn't mean to do it. I pushed the swing at her. I thought she'd catch it."

"It hit me in the head," Kristin whined.

"But I didn't mean to—"

"Okay. That's enough," Bev said. "Either play nice, or we'll go home."

Michael scampered off first. Finally Kristin unwound herself from her mother and headed back to the play area.

"Would you mind going over and keeping an eye on the kids a minute, Dale?" Bev asked, to cover her ploy to give him a piece of her mind away from his mother. "I'll be there in a minute."

He gave her a questioning look.

"You could play with them. They'd enjoy that," Dotty said.

Dale arched a brow at his mother, but did as Bev asked.

"Sorry to put you through that," Bev said, settling back on the bench. "I just need to get my wits about me before I talk with Michael. Sometimes he's so hard to handle, and I need to keep calm."

"Kids can be a handful," Dotty said. "It's much harder when you're alone. I always had Al to stand by me when we needed to discipline Dale, although he was a good boy most of the time."

Bev had a difficult time imagining Dale as a boy. She truly wondered if he'd ever really been one.

"I'd better rescue Dale," she said, rising. She marched across the grass, and as she neared, she beckoned Dale aside. "I wanted to talk with you away from your mother."

His face brightened. "You've thought of someone?"

Someone? When she realized he thought she had information about a caregiver, the awareness smoothed the edge of her anger, but she still had to speak her mind. "It's not about your mother. It's about my children." She drew him farther away from the kids so they wouldn't hear.

His expression darkened.

"It's obvious you don't like kids. I want—"

"I never said that." He glanced toward his mother then back to her.

She let her gaze drift to Dotty, trying to make their conversation appear to be genial. "I can see it in your actions." She tried to keep her voice low and controlled. "I really don't care how you feel, but I want you to know that I love my kids, and I don't expect you to discipline them."

"Look, Bev, I didn't—"

"You bellowed at Michael. That's my place, not yours. I can criticize my children, but you can't."

He stepped back. "Sorry, I just thought you were having a problem getting him to—"

She felt tears blur her eyes. "I have problems, yes, but I don't need your help. I can handle it myself."

"I've recently asked for your help." He gave a feeble gesture toward his mother. "I only thought…" His voice faded, then he rallied. "Sometimes people need someone else, but I hear you." He lifted his hand. "I'll stay clear of your kids."

"Good," she said, though she didn't feel good at all. She'd begun to like Dale.

"Why don't you go back to your mother, and let me take care of things here?"

Dale felt the sting of Bev's comment. He'd thought she would appreciate his making an effort to get Michael's attention. He guessed he'd been wrong.

He kicked a stone as he headed back toward his mother, hoping she hadn't spotted the tension that flashed like sparks from Bev's eyes. He'd called her a mother hen earlier. Mother tiger would have been more realistic.

The kicker was he liked Bev—a lot more than any woman he'd met in a long time, but that didn't change his attitude. Still, he'd hoped to remain on a friendly basis for his parents' sake.

The truth shimmered over him. His last thought was a coverup. She'd been growing on him, and if the blossoming friendship would have any hope of continuing, he needed to stay out of Bev's business. Yet something inside him wanted to help. The kids needed discipline— the boy especially—but both needed something more. Direction, he thought. Bev gave orders, but didn't seem to follow through. He could give her some good pointers. He faltered, knowing he'd better learn to keep quiet.

"Is Bev angry with you?" Dotty asked as soon as he reached her.

He grimaced, wondering how a woman with blurred eyesight could see so much.

"You shouldn't discipline her children, Dale. That's her business."

He opened his mouth to refute her comment, but she didn't give him a moment.

"She's a lovely woman," his mother said. "She's had a hard life."

Her words made Dale realize he knew little about Bev's life except she was a widowed mother. "How do you know about her life?"

"Women sense things, but I've also spoken with Millie. She comes by during the week to visit. She's a wonderful lady. I can see why your father thinks so much of her."

Mildred visited his mother during the week. That was something else he didn't know. "What about Bev's life?" Dale let his gaze drift to the playground slide. Bev stood at the bottom, waiting for Kristin to take a turn.

His mother ignored his question. "It's just sad when a young woman has such burdens. She should be enjoying life and sharing it with a husband."

"Seems like she should be concentrating on those kids before one of them gets killed."

"Dale, I can't believe you said that."

The disappointment in his mother's voice caused him to regret his comment.

"Where's your compassion?" she asked.

"I have compassion. I think they need a firm hand. And love," he added before his mother became upset again.

"Love is the answer," Dotty said.

His mother's eyes said more than he wanted to hear. She was conspiring, he guessed, working on a romance. His heart ached. She'd wanted grandchildren so badly, and he'd let down both his parents.

"Are you ready to go?" he asked, rather than plowing any further into a discussion about Bev.

"I suppose. It's getting a little chilly."

He stood, released the brake on her wheelchair and

shifted it around. Bev looked their way, and he lifted his hand in a wave. She barely responded.

"You should tell Bev we're leaving," Dotty said as he moved her chair along the sidewalk.

"I already did."

For a moment no one spoke until his mother, like a person who loves a song and keeps singing it over and over, started the topic again. "Bev needs a good husband—a man who'll love her and the children. Someone raised as a believer who can be faithful. Marriage is a wonderful experience when it's between two people whom God meant for each other."

What could he say that he hadn't already said? God had meant his father and mother to marry. They were a perfect couple. One of a kind. Dale didn't question that. But in his heart, he sensed the Lord was leading him to remain unattached. No troubles. No heartache.

Anyway, he'd make a lousy parent.

Chapter Four

Bev looked up as Annie DeWitt poked her head into the Loving Care playroom. "Dale Levin's here to see you." Her voice rose above the clamor of the children, and she gave Bev a conspiring smile.

Dale? Her pulse skipped for a moment before she realized something must be wrong. Bev's voice lodged in her throat as she brushed away Annie's insinuation with a wave of her hand and rose from her crouched position. "Don't start that, Annie."

Bev stepped over a toy truck as she headed for the doorway. "Can you keep an eye on things until I can send in someone else? It's almost time for me to leave anyway."

Annie took over, and Bev hurried to the front door, searching Dale's face for bad news. "What's wrong?" she asked.

Dale drew back, his expression becoming apologetic. "Nothing. I didn't realize I'd frighten you."

Relief washed over her followed by surprise. "Then why are you—"

"Impetuous, I suppose."

His grin rallied her pulse back to a skip.

"I recalled your saying you worked here, and I had a couple of things to talk over with you." Dale shoved his hands into his jacket pockets, his gaze surveying the room. "Is this a good time to talk?"

Addled by his sudden appearance, Bev calmed her thoughts and glanced at her watch. "I'm off in a couple of minutes, and my mom has Kristin today. That would probably be better."

He agreed and remained by the door.

As she walked away to say good-night to her employer, Christie Hanuman, Bev asked herself what she was doing. She was absolutely loony to build a friendship with Dale. She knew it, but something pushed her forward despite her reservations.

She hurried not to keep him waiting, and in minutes, Bev followed him outside and down the steps.

Dale gestured toward the highway. "How about Dee's Grill? It's right up the road. That is if you have the time."

"Fine," she said, her bewilderment growing. She pulled her car keys from her handbag. "Is this about your mother?"

"In part. But I also need a favor." He gave her a wave and headed for his car.

In part? A favor? His response unsettled her worse than not knowing at all. Bev climbed into her car, rolled onto the highway and, in moments, aimed her car into the small parking lot of the grill. Dale pulled in beside her. She exited the car and followed him to the entrance.

Inside they found a booth and ordered coffee. Bev felt puzzled and worried that he'd learned bad news about his mother.

In a moment the waitress returned with their drinks and a carafe. Dale thanked her, then settled back. "Thanks for seeing me on such short notice. I should have called you." He gazed at his coffee cup, and for the first time, Bev noticed his nervousness.

"You're welcome, but what's this about? Is your mother—" She paused, realizing she was moving into a sensitive area.

Her comment seemed to catch his attention, and his gaze settled on hers. "Mom's the same. What I really need is your help."

She raised an eyebrow, her curiosity soaring. "Help with what?"

"My mother's care."

"You want me to take care of your mother?"

He shook his head. "No. Not you. How about your mother? You know Dad isn't willing to admit Mom into a facility."

"Yes," she said, only imagining how she might feel in his shoes. "It would be a difficult decision."

Dale's downcast head bobbed with agreement. "I don't want that either." He raised his eyes and gave her a direct look. "But he doesn't want to hire anyone either because he doesn't want to hire a stranger." He released a ragged sigh. "So I've been thinking about your mother."

"I noticed your look the other night. I had the same thought, but I don't know about that, Dale."

His hopeful look faded. "She's a nurse and has spare time. Mom mentioned she's been dropping by for visits. Do you think she might be willing to help my dad?"

"That's up to my mom. When she came to Loving, she stressed that now she had time to enjoy her retirement and renew old friendships. I'm not sure she'd want to give up that freedom."

Her expression must have jarred him. Dale's look sank to discouragement. "I know it's a lot to ask, but they seem like such good friends. Your mother wouldn't be a stranger in my dad's eyes."

Bev's heart ached for him and the sad situation. Dale's ill-humored behavior softened in her thoughts as she listened to his concern and love for his family. Underneath his gruffness was a soft-hearted man. He needed to open up and let it out.

"When my mom said those things, she didn't know about your mother, and she hadn't run into your dad yet.

That might make a difference. I could suggest it to her. Would that help?"

A look of relief spread across Dale's face. "If you would, I'd be eternally grateful." He leaned across the tabletop, slid his hand over hers and gave it a squeeze.

The warmth rushed up her arm and prickled down her back. She searched his eyes, amazed at the depth of emotion she saw. He was bound so tightly with restrictive behaviors Bev wasn't sure Dale even knew the feelings were there.

A thought traveled through her. She wanted to know this man, to see his potential as a loving person, to know why he held himself aloof from showing his feelings. More than once, she'd observed his compassion and his fear. He tried to conceal them even from himself, but he couldn't hide them from Bev. She'd spent years obscuring her own secret hurts. She was a master.

His hand remained on hers, and Bev didn't move. How long had it been since a man had touched her hand in such an intimate way? She couldn't remember. She studied Dale's worried face. His beautiful eyes were darkened with concern, the deep-blue color like a stormy sea.

"I can't thank you enough, Bev," Dale said, breaking the silence. "Being an only child, I have no one to turn to, no one to be a sounding board for my thoughts, no one who cares. It's nice having a person willing to listen."

Bev watched a faint grin form on his face as he gave her hand a final squeeze and drew it back to lift his coffee cup.

"I suppose this seems silly to you. You hardly know me, and I'm asking for your help. It's not like me. I usually handle things on my own."

She knew him better than he realized. In her opinion, he didn't handle things well at all. "I'll take it as a compliment that you trust me enough to ask," Bev said.

"You're a nice lady, Bev. You're a beautiful person."

Her pulse did another waltz up her arm, and the sensation irritated her. She didn't want to react to this man's attention—or any man's, for that matter.

"You're beautiful inside and out." His gaze washed over her.

Bev didn't know what to say. She sensed he was sweet-talking her, and it was working. Her stomach had joined her pulse, and the two danced a jig through her body until she felt unable to calm her emotions. She shook her head. "I try to be kind. Kindness looks beautiful."

"You're that, too." He reached for the carafe.

She watched him add coffee to the cups, then take a sip as if his mind had flown off somewhere else. She needed the reprieve to calm herself, to get things back into perspective. Her emotions had been doing push-ups since Dale touched her hand.

Bev eyed her watch. "I suppose I'd better get home."

Dale turned his head and checked the wall clock. "I didn't realize so much time had passed. I still have that favor to ask."

"Favor? I thought you'd asked it."

"I had two favors to ask."

Two? She noted an uncomfortable look edging across his face.

"This one is more personal," he said.

Personal? Her kids came to mind, and she girded herself for an argument. If he was going to tell her to keep her children away from his parents or how to raise them, she'd let him have it right now, no matter how sweet he was somewhere inside his hard head. "Is this about my children?"

His head snapped upward. "No. Not at all."

No? She slipped her hands into her lap, embarrassed by her thoughts.

"Ian Barry, an old high-school friend, invited me to dinner tomorrow night."

Hearing the name gave her a start. "I know Ian and Esther from church."

His face brightened. "You do? Great."

Bev had no idea where this favor was going. A proper hostess gift? What?

"Ian suggested I bring someone along. I thought of you."

Bev's heart skipped a beat. "That's because I'm the only woman you know in town."

"No, I—"

"I'm only kidding." She lowered her gaze and looked into her cup while pondering the possibility. She'd been out of the social loop for so long. Too long, her mother thought.

She let her response settle in her thoughts a moment before answering. "I like Ian and Esther. I'd be glad to go to dinner if my mom will watch the kids."

Bev heard her mother pulling into the driveway. Mildred had been out with another old friend, and Bev realized she was truly enjoying her retirement. "Did you have fun?" Bev asked when she came through the doorway.

Mildred dropped her handbag onto the table and settled into a recliner. "I did. It was like old times. Seems nice to have so much freedom."

Bev's heart sank, thinking of Dale's request.

"I stopped to look at an apartment today," Mildred said, "but I didn't like it. It was on the second floor."

Bev was grateful her fears of two women under one roof had gone unfounded. "Take your time," she said, wondering how to broach the topic of Dotty. She finally took the roundabout way. "Dale Levin stopped by Loving Care today."

Her mother's head flew up like a startled bird. "Really? Something wrong?"

"No. Dotty's the same." She lost her courage and

segued to a different topic. "He asked me out to dinner tomorrow night."

"A real date? I'm thrilled."

"Not really. It's a favor." She explained the situation and hoped her mother wouldn't try to make something of it. "I need a baby-sitter if you're willing."

"Certainly I'll watch the kids," Mildred said while a coy smile rose to her lips. "Are you sure this is a favor and not a date?"

Bev held up her hand. "Don't start matchmaking, Mom."

"Dotty and I both think you'd make a great couple. Don't push the idea out of your head, Bev. You just never know."

Before Bev could respond, her mother shifted forward on the edge of her chair.

"Speaking of Dotty, I went to see her today. She's not doing well. My heart breaks for the whole family."

The topic gave Bev an opportunity to introduce Dale's request. "Me, too. Al could really use some help."

"I know, and that's why I'm thinking I should offer to take care of Dotty."

Bev tried to hide her surprise. "Dale's been trying to get Al to hire someone. I'm sure they'd be grateful."

"Not hire. Volunteer."

Volunteer? "But that's a tremendous commitment, Mom."

Mildred eased deeper into the chair and nodded. "I

know. I've been praying about it, and I read something in the Bible the other day that made me think about this." She rose. "Let me get it."

Her mother hurried from the room while Bev sat, amazed at the turn of events. More of God's work, she guessed. Yet she worried about the volunteering part. Certainly her mother could use some extra money to keep her independence and help with her living expenses.

Mildred returned, carrying the Bible. "It's in Philippians." She fingered through the pages until she located the passage. "Here it is. 'Each of you should look not only to your own interests, but also to the interests of others. Your attitude should be the same as that of Christ Jesus.'" She lowered the Bible and looked at Bev. "That really spoke to me."

"It's easier said than done."

"Yes, in some ways it is." She paused, her gaze drifting across the room. "Al and I were talking the other day and laughed about a pact we'd made each other years ago that we'd always be friends, and even if we were apart, if we needed each other, we'd find a way to be there."

"Mom, you said that when you were kids."

"I know, but we made a pact, and see what the Lord has done? He's guided me back to Loving so I could keep my promise, just like the Lord kept His."

"God is different than people. I know the Levins need help. Dale's said the same, but I don't want you to say you can do something that you can't. What I don't like is your volunteering. It should be a paid position."

"That's my decision, Bev. I don't need the money. Your dad left me well-cared for, and my retirement benefits are fine. That's not my concern. What I pray is before I commit to anything, I want to make sure I can handle the responsibility." Mildred looked at her with thoughtful eyes.

Bev reprimanded herself for her reaction to her mother's wish. Bev had promised Dale she'd help, and now she'd tried to discourage her mother. Her promise had been an empty one. But why? The answer struck her. She feared her mother would get so busy with the Levins she'd forget about looking for an apartment and lose her interest in the children. Bev's reaction had been selfish.

"I know commitments are difficult," Mildred continued. "You have the kids and so you don't do much for yourself."

"I have since you've been here. It's given me more time for myself." The truth of her admission poked at her.

"I look at you and wonder what's going to happen. You're so tied up with the kids you have no life of your own."

Bev saw it coming again.

"No husband. You're too young to be alone." She lowered her eyes. "It's not just me, Bev. Dotty would like to see you and Dale get together. She so wants to know he's happily married before—"

"Mom, we've already talked about this. I find Dale an intriguing man. I like many things about him, but he's not crazy about kids, and he has no interest in marriage. Anyway, he's just not my type."

"What is your type?" her mother asked.

Bev gazed at her while the question rolled around in her head. She closed her eyes, almost ashamed that she no longer saw Jesse's face. The vision she saw was Dale and his haunting eyes.

Chapter Five

Dale opened the passenger door for Bev. "You look amazing," he said, admiring her knit top the color of new grass. She wore a flowery print skirt that reminded him of a spring meadow.

Meadows and new grass. He cringed, hearing himself blathering poetry. When he'd seen her at her front door, he'd been startled to find himself nervous as a teenager on his first date. And this wasn't a date.

Bev thanked him and climbed into his car. He closed the passenger door and rounded the trunk to the driver's side, slid in and turned the key in the ignition. When he shifted to look out the rear window, Bev's golden hair brushed against her shoulders and glinted in the setting sun. She really was beautiful.

Dale backed out of the driveway, and once on the highway, he pulled his thoughts from her to the question that had niggled at him since he'd spoken with her at the grill. "Did you have a chance to talk with your mother?"

"Actually, she spoke to me first," Bev said.

"About caring for my mom?"

"Uh-huh. She's praying about it. She always asks God for guidance."

Since his mother's illness, Dale had never asked God's help for anything. "Do you ask God for direction?"

"I do, but I don't always listen. I would handle things much better if I did."

Though he smiled at her response, he felt envy. He'd lost the impetus to pray, and he'd harbored so much anger at the Lord he'd become stubborn, though he knew it was a sin. "My folks pray. We grew up saying bedtime prayers and blessings at the table. I don't anymore."

Bev's head swiveled toward him. "Why not?"

"Long story. Let's not go there tonight."

Her puzzled expression turned to disappointment, and he knew changing the subject was a must. "I'm amazed your mother brought up the topic first. The co-incidence seems uncanny."

"It's not uncanny, Dale. That's how the Lord works. He sets wheels in motion so that our free will spots a need and we respond. It's what people do. Christians give the credit to God."

Dale gave the credit to Millie and her soft heart.

"Her praying about it sounds hopeful."

Bev nodded, and Dale realized that his earlier admission had undone the easy conversation they'd been sharing. He wanted to kick himself.

"I'm sorry you don't believe in prayer," Bev said.

His mind went blank. What could he say? "After being kicked around by God a few times, I just gave up."

"It's not God that kicks us, Dale. It's the evil in the world. The Lord's willing to take our hand if we ask. I've had a few kicks myself, but that's another story."

He wanted to know the story, but the look on her face told him to tread lightly. "Maybe I've been rash," he said to appease her.

"I'd say so. You need to open your heart."

"If he had one," Dale could almost hear her saying. He reached across the distance and brushed her hand. "Thanks for putting up with me. I won't deny I have things to learn, and you're a good teacher." He gave her fingers a squeeze, loving the feeling of her slender hand beneath his.

"It's nice to hear you say that. We all have things to learn."

His chest tightened, seeing her tender smile.

Ian's house appeared, and Dale pulled into the driveway. He hurried around the car to open Bev's door, and as she alighted, a sweet flowery scent drifted past him. She reminded him of springtime and lilacs.

As they headed up the sidewalk, Ian opened the door

and stepped onto the porch to greet them. "Glad you could make it," he said, "and, Bev, this is a nice surprise. I didn't realize you two knew each other."

Dale explained as they entered the house, welcomed by an appetizing aroma that filled the hallway. "Dinner smells wonderful."

"Esther's handiwork," Ian said. "Come into the living room."

Dale rested his hand against Bev's back, guiding her through the archway behind Ian and feeling the warmth of her body beneath her shirt. When he sat on the sofa, Bev joined him and the closeness washed over him. He'd never before felt a connection with any woman as he did with Bev.

"I'll be with you in a minute," Ian said and hurried from the room.

The wait was short. Ian came into the room carrying a plate of appetizers with Esther behind him, carrying their child.

Dale rose, feeling awkward for some reason. He knew he should make some cute-baby comment, but it didn't feel right.

Esther gave them both a welcoming smile. "Hi, Bev." She turned toward him. "And you must be Dale. Good to have you both here."

Dale grasped her free hand in greeting.

Ian beamed as he motioned to his son. "This is Tyler. He's just turned one."

"He's so cute," Bev said, reaching out to tickle the boy. "I see him in church all the time. He's always so good."

"He's teething," Esther said. "So we never know these days."

They sat, and Ian passed the hors d'oeuvres. Dale took some kind of crescent roll-up with a paper napkin, and when Ian sat, the conversation began. The subject drifted from topic to topic until it settled on Dale's mother. Immediately, he tried to think of something to change the subject.

"You've got some boy there," he said, figuring that should do it. He clapped his hands to get the child's attention, amazing himself that he'd chosen the baby as his topic rather than anything else.

"You can hold him," Ian said, picking up the boy and carrying him over to Dale.

Dale watched, amazed, as Ian plopped the baby into his lap. "Hello, there, Tyler," he said, bouncing the child on his knee while trying to look as if he'd done it a million times. He glanced at Bev, aware that she probably guessed he was miserable.

The baby let out some gurgling noises while a smile grew on his lips. Before Dale noticed, a stream of drool rolled from Tyler's mouth and dripped onto his hands. He fought the look of disgust that he felt rising to his face.

"Sorry," Esther said. "That's part of teething."

She moved to rise, but Bev jumped up first and grasped the cloth from Esther's hands. She moved toward them and wiped the baby's mouth, then Dale's hands. Her smile looked so warm it touched Dale's heart.

"Can I hold him?" she asked, giving him a private wink.

"If you must," Dale said, hoping she knew he was kidding. Relief washed over him as Bev lifted Tyler and sat beside him again. But reality struck him, too. If he ever, heaven forbid, took the plunge, he'd have to face being a parent.

Dale shifted his attention to Bev, cuddling Tyler. The boy cooed and grasped at her long hair before yanking at her small hoop earring. Bev didn't blink an eye. She kept talking and unwound the baby's hand, then gave his chubby fist a kiss. She was a born mother.

The revelation raked through him like salt on a wound. He and Bev were totally incompatible. She loved children. He tolerated them at best. She deserved a man excited at the thought of being a father. The unwanted awareness stabbed him. If that were so, what was he doing in this oil-and-water situation?

Dale swivelled in his desk chair and looked out his office window at the Grand Rapids skyline. On Friday, he'd head back to Loving for a long Memorial Day weekend. He felt unsettled, as if he were on a pulley being yanked back and forth between the two cities and, most of the time, suspended in the air.

Home had always been a word that meant comfort and security, but in the past couple of years as he'd watched his mother decline with nothing he or anyone could do, home had become a heavy burden. Yet his father's love for his mother had never wavered.

Love was a strange thing—a blend of joy and contentment, yet always on the brink of heartache. He'd faced it over and over while his mother's life was ebbing away. He could do nothing to help her, nothing to stop her. She'd given her all to him, and he'd been a failure to her. Pain surged through him; he already felt the grief and loss he and his father would both feel.

Life seemed easier without all that. Lonely, maybe, and purposeless at times, but safer. Though angry with God, Dale knew the Bible. He'd been raised in the faith, and he sensed his parents had that perfect love he'd read about in scripture, the kind of love beyond his understanding. He'd never find a love like that nor would he want to.

As soon as the thought shot through him, a vision of Bev filled his head. He spun back toward his desk, wanting to rid himself of springtime and flowers, the meandering ruminations that filled his mind so often. He needed to get to work and not waste time with his head in the clouds.

He'd asked himself before why his mind was always wending its way to Bev, and he'd already decided it was to camouflage his fears. Thinking of Bev's pretty face, her enchanting smile that brightened a room, seemed so

much better than picturing his mother's gloomy bedroom and her misery.

The phone's ring jerked him from his thoughts. The
voice on the other end of the line startled him.

"It's Bev. I hope I'm not disturbing you."

The thoughts he'd just brushed aside floated back.
"No. Not at all. I'm surprised to hear from you." The vi-
sions rose again, Bev's golden hair, her lovely cheekbones
that drew his attention to her ever-changing hazel eyes.

"I got your telephone number from your dad."

His chest tightened. "Is something wrong at home?"

"No. Nothing like that. I'm in Grand Rapids, and I
thought maybe I could stop by your place when I'm finished. I've never seen your apartment."

"You're here? Now?"

She chuckled. "Christie Hanuman needed someone
to pick up supplies for Loving Care and I volunteered.
It's like a half day off with pay."

He heard the smile in her voice.

"I'd like to see you." He felt a grin of his own. "I'll
make dinner."

"I can't stay that long."

"We'll see," he said, giving her directions. When he
hung up the phone, he fell back against the chair. Bev
in Grand Rapids. Bev at his apartment. Bev in his world.

Bev stood on the apartment stoop and pushed the bell
beneath Dale's name. She heard a resounding buzz,

caught the door handle and opened the door. She headed for the elevator, and when it arrived, she pushed the button for the tenth floor.

She couldn't believe she'd been this nervy. It had taken her an hour to collect the courage to call Dale, even though she'd planned it.

Bev figured having a look at a man's apartment might give her clues to who he really was and what he liked. So many questions had filled her head since the last time she'd seen Dale. Bev didn't know why she felt so driven to save Dale from himself. Since she'd visited his family's home, she'd witnessed many of his fine qualities—his love and concern for his parents, his thoughtfulness, his devotion. She knew he was a man worth saving.

What troubled her was his relationship with God. What made her curious was his attitude toward children and marriage. He'd related his viewpoint more than once. Bev wanted to understand and to help him see things differently—not for herself, but for him and whoever he might fall in love with one day. The image charged through her like a volt.

The apartment elevator swished open, and Bev stepped into the carpeted hallway. She checked the wall sign, saw his number and turned left toward the front of the building.

His hello sailed from his doorway to greet her, and she felt a smile blossom on her face, like that of a teenager gaping at the boy of her dreams. Bev couldn't believe she'd lost control of her senses.

"Hi," she said, reaching him. To her surprise, he bent down and kissed her cheek. A hot flush crept up her neck, and she averted her face so he wouldn't notice. "Nice place," she said, blabbering comments while trying to calm herself.

The apartment was attractive—masculine colors, but open and warm with wide windows letting in the sinking sun. He had a leather sofa and matching love seat situated for conversation but also for a view of the city through the glass. Lights had begun to come on in the surrounding buildings, and Bev figured that at night the sight would leave her with a lonely feeling.

"Please," Dale said, his arm sweeping the length of the room. "Have a seat."

She dropped her handbag on a nearby chair and wandered toward the view. "You can look out on the world here." And hide from it, she thought.

"The sunsets are nice," he said.

His response made her wonder if he liked the view all that much. "Is it lonely?"

She saw him lift his shoulders, his gaze still directed through the window. "I'm used to being alone."

Alone and lonely were two different things, she thought.

Dale turned to face her. "I suppose you don't know what that's like."

"Not with two kids," she said, but she did know lone-liness. Children didn't take the place of having another person with whom to share her joys and sorrows or a man to hold her in his arms at night.

"Would you like a soda? Coffee? And I meant my offer about dinner. If you don't trust my cooking, we can go out."

She shook her head and pulled her gaze from the sky-line. "Thanks. I really can't stay long."

He gave her a curious look, and she could hear his mind asking the question—why was she there?

Bev wandered across the room to the saddle-col-ored sofa. Its lingering aroma aroused her senses as she settled onto the leather cushions. She ran her hand over the smooth surface, willing her nerves to subside. She felt giddy with amazement that she'd proposed the visit.

Dale sat in a chair nearby. His fingers played along the upholstered arm, admitting by his action he felt as uneasy as she did.

As the silence lingered, Dale bounded from the chair. "I'll make a pot of coffee."

He vanished through a doorway, and Bev rose, de-ciding to follow. She entered the kitchen as he was spooning grounds into the coffeemaker.

"I don't mean to surprise you, Dale. Besides being curious about your apartment—which is very nice, by the way—I wanted to talk about a couple of things."

He took a slow turn toward her, the coffee scoop suspended. "I figured, but I'm not sure what this is about."

Neither did she, really. She sank onto a kitchen chair at a small table for two. No room for kids here, she thought, as her attention drifted to the practical, tidy layout of the room. At least he was neat. She'd learned that.

"We've been thrust together," Bev said, her gaze drifting to his puzzled face, "and I figure we might as well make the most of it by being friends, and I figured I should get to know you better."

"No problem from me."

"We've had our differences, but I hoped we've resolved some of them."

Dale hit the button on the coffeemaker, then drew up a chair, swiveled it around and sat facing her. "Okay. Let's be friends. It makes sense." Though he said the words, she wondered if he were questioning the wisdom.

"Give me a question," he said. "What do you want to know?" He reached across the distance and rested a hand on her arm. "And this is not one-sided. I can ask questions, too."

"Fair," she said, wishing she could refuse, but knowing she couldn't. Still, no one said she had to reveal the whole truth. Half the story wouldn't exactly be lying.

Dale eased forward and rested his arms against the chair back.

She collected her thoughts and decided to begin with

her main concern. "What bothers me the most is your attitude toward God."

Bev noticed him cringe with her comment, but she barreled along. "Your parents are obviously Christians. You were raised in the faith. So what happened?"

"That's difficult to answer."

She sensed he was being evasive and waited, her eyes searching his.

"It's obvious, I suppose. My mother and father have been the best. They've given me more than I can repay. I consider their relationship perfect. I believe that for each person there's one soul mate, one special person and no other."

"You mean once you fall in love that's it?"

"Yes," he said. "If God directs us, then we're led to that one person He meant for us."

Her heart skipped at the thought. She and Jesse? That couldn't have been God's guidance. "I disagree, Dale. Do you remember that God gives us free will. I told you a few days ago that I ask for God's direction, but I don't always listen. That's wrong, but it's part of our human sinfulness. We make bad choices sometimes. I don't blame the Lord for that."

"Well, I do. He's almighty. Omniscient."

"But he's not a tyrant. He gives us freedom to choose."

"That was God's mistake."

Bev recoiled. His comment felt like a slap.

"I'm sorry, Bev. I've shocked you. I don't know if God really listens to everyone. He's dealing with war and famine, dying and birth. Why listen to me? So why should I listen to Him?"

Bev's heart broke, hearing his honesty.

"When my mother was diagnosed with MS, I spent so much time in prayer. I begged and pleaded, but my mom has gone downhill. I've seen no mercy. How can I love a God who does that to one of the sweetest women in the world?"

"God has promised us love, forgiveness and salvation. He is plenteous in mercy, Scripture tells us, but we don't see the big picture, Dale. We don't know why things happen. I blame the world's sin and evil on Satan, not God. The devil undermines the Lord's work in every way, and not because the Lord isn't powerful, but because He's created us in His likeness. He's given us that free will that I mentioned before. We make bad choices."

Dale's eyes narrowed as if he were searching Bev's soul, and she held her breath.

"I don't know, Bev. I just know what I feel."

"It's okay to feel anger and frustration. I do that with my kids all the time, but I don't stop loving them. We're God's children, and he never stops loving us." She made a quick glance around the room, figuring the look was futile. "I don't suppose you have a Bible handy."

His head snapped upward. "I do."

Her heart skipped and filled with hope. "Could I see it?"

He rose without comment and headed into the hallway. Bev sat suspended, praying she could find the verse she wanted to share.

In moments, he returned carrying a well-worn black leather Bible. "This was my grandfather's," he said.

Disappointment shuffled through her. She'd hoped perhaps he'd been the one to dog-ear the pages. She extended her hand. "It's in Hebrews, if I remember correctly."

"That's in the New Testament," he said.

He knew it was the New Testament, and she smiled. If he knew that much, maybe he knew even more. She prayed his faith hadn't drifted too far off course. Being angry at God and being an unbeliever weren't the same.

As her thoughts piled one on the other, she flipped through the pages, scanning the verses. "Here it is in the tenth chapter. 'Let us hold unswervingly to the hope we profess, for he who promised is faithful.'" She lifted her gaze to Dale's before continuing. "'And let us consider how we may spur one another on toward love and good deeds.'"

She lowered the Bible. "God's promises are sure. Instead of fighting the life he gave us, the Lord's asking us to make the most of it, to help each other and to show love not anger. He has promised that He'll be with us. His promise is a sure thing."

He reached toward her, his hand open, and she slipped the Bible into it. He stared at the page in silence, perhaps rereading the Scripture she'd read aloud. She knew the Bible held so many other messages, but with her own lack of Bible study, she didn't know where they were. She thought of Job and Jonah, men whose lives fell apart but their faith kept them strong. They never stopped praying or gave up hope.

"Thanks," Dale said finally. He placed the Bible on the lamp table beside him. "Maybe I'd better start reading this."

Bev's spirit calmed as if a fresh breeze had drifted over her. "I'm glad. God is forgiving and His love endures forever. It's just difficult for us to believe that a love can be that strong."

"My dad and mom have a love like that," Dale said. "I admire them. I'd never find a relationship like theirs. Never."

Bev drew back while a comment bounced in her head. It wasn't the time to say it, but if he treated children as he did and snapped people's heads off at a touchy topic, he was correct. Who needed that?

Then another idea crossed her mind. If Dale felt that way, could that be why he'd never married? She had so many more questions to ask, but not today. She didn't want to thwart what the Holy Spirit had accomplished in their short time together. Even one step forward lifted Bev's heart.

"The coffee," Dale said, rising. "I forgot about it."

The scent drifted to meet Bev, too. "I really should go." She rose and took a step toward the doorway.

Dale moved to her side and captured her arms. "Why hurry?" His eyes searched hers, leaving her addled.

"It's almost dark. My mom will wonder where I am."

"I have a telephone," he said.

He stood so close she could smell the subtle fragrance of his aftershave. Her hands became clammy, and she felt out of her element. Standing together in his apartment seemed too intimate, too personal.

She drew back to explain, but instead he drew her into his arms and pressed his cheek against her hair. "Thank you," he murmured. "I'm glad you came."

"You're welcome." She forced herself out of his embrace, wanting to stay there, but sensing his attention was like a whirlpool. If she didn't fight the pull, she'd be lost.

She stepped away, but he captured her hand. "I haven't asked you my questions yet. Remember?"

Bev lifted her arm to check her watch and saw her hands tremble. "Next time."

A tender smile drifted across his face. "Next weekend. Dad said you're coming over for Memorial Day."

He hadn't released her left hand, and she felt him squeeze her fingers. Her small hand seemed lost in his larger one.

"I'll see you then with my questions ready," he said.

"Great." She'd hoped to sound casual, but she was far from it. Bev slid her hand from his grasp, but the pressure of his touch remained, just as Dale always stayed in her thoughts long after he'd vanished from her sight.

Chapter Six

"Dale, why don't you play ball with Michael?" Dotty asked.

Dale's back stiffened as he heard his mother's voice, and he focused on the back of his parents' yard. Michael ambled across the grass, looking bored. The boy tossed a ball into the air, catching it some of the time. Better than throwing it at his sister, Dale figured.

"You don't have to," Bev said, as if she could read his mind.

Bev's eyes reflected the hurt she felt when he ignored her children. He didn't know why he felt as he did. He'd never had much experience and felt inept, a feeling he didn't like.

He pulled himself from his thoughts and got up from his chair. He wanted to remind her he was in charge of the grill, but he realized the boy needed attention. If Michael didn't get positive attention, he went for the negative, and it always worked. He got what he wanted. The boy had a penchant for getting into trouble. He'd already been reprimanded for tossing a ball and nearly hitting his grandmother. Good old Millie had just tossed it back without a comment, but Bev hadn't let it stop there.

Dale had watched Kristin, too, but she seemed better-behaved. She'd spent most of the time drawing pictures for everyone.

Dale crossed the yard to Michael. "Want to play catch?"

Michael shrugged, but Dale hadn't missed the look of interest in the boy's face.

"Do you have a glove?"

Michael shook his head.

Dale put up a finger and sprinted for the garage. He remembered seeing a couple of his old baseball mitts hanging on a peg. He'd thought they'd be hard as steel, but to his surprise, they weren't half bad. He carried them into the yard and tossed one to Michael.

The boy caught it and slid it on his hand. Dale chuckled. The mitt was too big, but Michael eyed it and smacked his fist into the palm as he'd probably seen the ballplayers do on TV.

"Ready?" Dale asked.

Michael played the part. He whacked his glove again and waited for Dale to pitch.

He threw a slow straight ball to give the kid half a

chance. Michael fumbled, but Dale knew it was because of the oversize glove.

Dale caught the boy's ragged pitch, then threw another. As the ball sailed back and forth, sometimes bouncing to the ground, Dale sent his mind back in time, trying to recall how he'd felt at age eight. Free, important and know-it-all. His parents' only child was spoiled to the core. Dale wondered if that was his problem today. No one paid him quite as much attention as his parents had. Recently, Bev was running a close second. Dale wondered if it weren't his mind playing tricks on him. In truth, he was the one preoccupied.

"Nice job," Al said, crossing the lawn and giving the boy a thumbs-up. In the past minutes, Michael had shown improvement at catching the ball.

The boy's eyes lit up with the compliment, and Dale saw his pride. Kind words worked wonders.

"Did you see him shag that one?" Dale asked.

His father nodded.

"Show him how to throw a knuckle ball, Dad. I was never good at that." Dale walked toward his dad with the ball extended.

Al took it and ambled to the boy. "Look here," he said, demonstrating how to position his fingers. "When you can throw a good knuckle ball, you confuse the batter. The ball flutters all over the place."

"You mean like this?" Michael grasped the ball and

demonstrated by waving it through the air as he darted toward Dale.

Dale held out his arms to halt him, but the boy charged into his embrace. The action shocked Dale. He hadn't planned to hug the boy, but he certainly couldn't reject him now. The child stood back, looking as startled as Dale felt.

Dale sent the boy a pleasant look, hoping to waylay the child's embarrassment. "Can you throw him a few, Dad? I think the fire's ready for the steaks."

Al nodded, probably enjoying a chance to spend time with a child—not a grandchild, but a reasonable facsimile in his mind.

Bev sat back, reveling in the lovely day. She'd relived her short visit with Dale the past Thursday and felt good about their talk. She really liked him, and trying to cover her feelings made her feel stressed. Now, at least, they'd come away from that afternoon with an agreement— friendship. Even more than that, she'd been ecstatic when he'd mentioned needing to read the Bible. If she had accomplished nothing else, Dale's admission filled her with joy.

Though his attention that day had made her uneasy, she'd decided it had been a natural response to their growing amicable relationship. Friendship was best for them both. He obviously wasn't looking for marriage and neither was she.

But companionship was another thing. Having someone to go to a movie with, to enjoy a play or walk in the park with seemed like a possibility now. She'd had a nice time with him at Ian's. Every time they'd been together without the kids had been pleasant.

She watched him now as he headed for the grill. He'd been so kind to entertain Michael, even if it was at his mother's prodding.

Dotty and her mother were deep in conversation. Bev could see the weakness in Dotty's face. Yet the woman was strong in faith. Her mother could make Dotty smile, which to Bev was a true gift of the spirit.

Bev rose and headed across the grass. A warm breeze fluttered through her hair, and she pushed her hair back before tucking a loose strand behind her ear. Dale's brown hair had lightened in the past couple of weeks as the sun had bleached it with highlights, and he looked relaxed and as sunny as the day.

When she approached, his eyes crinkled into a smile, and she pressed her hand against her chest for a moment, addled by the sensation she felt.

"Can I help?" she asked.

He grinned. "Sure. Talk to me."

"Why?" Immediately she feared he wanted to ask those questions she'd promised to answer.

"Talk or sing. Anything to entertain me while I make you the best steak you've had in ages."

"That's easy. I can't afford steak so even shoe leather would taste good to me."

"I like your sense of humor. Did I ever tell you that?"

"No." She paused a moment, wondering if she should be so honest. "Want me to tell you what I like about you?"

He drew back and cocked his head. "Sure."

"It's your eyes."

He looked at her and crossed them.

She'd never seen him so silly. She gave him a playful punch. "You have beautiful eyes. They're blue and deep like a whirlpool that draws me in. I feel as if I'm drowning."

"And you like that?"

He made her laugh. "It's the look, not the drowning." She turned away, then back with a new thought. "And you love your family. That's something I respect and admire." She gave his arm a squeeze. "And that's all you get."

"Whew! That's enough." He turned a steak, then looked up. "I'll give you your list later."

Her list? Her pulse skipped. She wondered what he might say, but her heart sank as she recalled his other list—the personal questions he'd promised to ask her.

Dale motioned toward the house. "These are nearly done. You can bring out the rest of the food."

Bev walked away, feeling uplifted yet scared. She liked this whole friendship idea. She only hoped her heart cooperated with the agreement.

Bev leaned back against the chair, the sun blocked by the large umbrella. The sense of family washed over her. She loved it and feared it. One day when her mother wasn't needed and the freshness of her and Al's redis-covered friendship had faded, the relationship would fade, too. Lately, thinking of the Levins seemed to give Bev a sense of purpose, and Dale had offered her a lit-tle excitement in her usual life.

"Three cheers for the cook," Mildred said, holding up her lemonade glass toward Dale. "The steaks were delicious."

"And thanks for all the food you brought," Al said. "I haven't enjoyed a day like this in a long time." He sank into a chair beside Mildred and folded his hands.

The saddest part of the day was Dotty's absence. She'd gone back to bed shortly after dinner, and Bev missed her gracious charm and undying spirit.

Bev eyed the table filled with dishes and silverware. She rose and grasped two serving bowls. "The kids are enjoying that game you found so I'll let you keep an eye on them while I clean up."

"I'll be glad to help," Mildred said, pushing herself up from her chair.

"No, Mom, please, you relax. This won't take long."

"I'll help her," Dale said, rising and piling the soiled plates into a stack.

Mildred didn't argue and settled back into her chair. Bev gathered an armload and Dale followed.

Al watched them clear the table. He'd covered his feelings all day while Dale and Dotty were there. With

Millie he could be honest. He watched Dale and Bev disappear into the house, and his heart lifted. He wondered, hoped that maybe the Lord had brought the two together for a deeper purpose. When he shifted his gaze to Millie, he let out a sigh so ragged it rattled through him.

"It's getting so difficult, Millie. It hurts me right here," Al said, pressing his hand against his chest. "I love her so much."

"I know you do." She reached out and patted his arm. "I felt the same when I lost my husband, but you know, life goes on, as they say. In time you adjust."

Al looked at her, remembering how pretty she was as a young woman. Yet he could still admire the matured version she was now. "Sometimes it's unbearably lonely."

"It is," Millie agreed.

"I've wanted someone to talk with for so long. Then you came back into my life." He shifted in his chair. "I can't talk with Dale very well. He doesn't want to deal with the emotion. Yet, he's been a good son. So faithful to us. So concerned."

"I'm happy to see Bev and Dale get along so well, but Bev tells me they're only friends."

Al gave her a grin. "The best marriages are made of friends first, then romance. You agree, Millie?"

"I agree."

"Funny, we never got serious about each other," Al said. "Dotty said the same to me."

"I valued your friendship more than romance. Those were a dime a dozen. Good friends are a blessing. And speaking of friendship, I've been thinking."

He listened as Millie read his heart. She knew he needed her, and here she was volunteering to care for Dotty.

"I'd like to relieve your mind," she said when she was finished.

"Millie," he said, searching her eyes. "You're a gift from the Lord. I don't know how long she has, but…" He choked on his words and couldn't finish.

"I'd feel blessed to help you if you'll have me."

"You're the answer to my prayers. I'll talk it over with Dotty. She's always been our orchestrator, the one who made sure everyone was taken care of. Nowadays she has so little control over anything, I want to let her make every decision I can."

"Yes, that's the right thing to do."

"So little I can do," he said. He rested his palm against Millie's arm and gave it a squeeze. His words of thanks had caught in his throat and if he forced them out, he'd embarrass himself with tears.

The Lord is my strength, Al repeated in his head as they sat in silence.

Bev glanced out the Levins' kitchen window to check on the children. She saw her mother and Al deep in conversation, and though she was curious, she went back to the sink. She scraped and rinsed while Dale slid dishes into the dishwasher. Occasionally, she glanced out the kitchen window to check on the children and was pleased to see them playing peacefully.

"Kristin's birthday is coming up. I think I'll look for that toss game. They seem to enjoy it."

"They're being good," Dale said, so near her he made her jump.

She turned and found him close enough to breathe in his distinctive aftershave. She needed to guard herself. "By the way, thanks for playing catch with Michael."

Dale shifted back a little, giving her breathing room.

"He needs a lot of attention," Dale said. "I watched him eat it up today when my dad and I were playing with him."

Bev felt herself shrink with his words. She could be a good parent, but she could never replace Jesse.

Dale tilted her chin upward and looked in her eyes as if he knew what she was thinking. "You can't be everything to him, Bev. He's a boy, and boys are different. Boys need more direction."

She nodded and tried to ease around him, but he didn't move.

"Look at Kristin. She's a girl and you're all she needs."

"I wouldn't say that, but I'm all she's got." She shifted her gaze out the window again. "I don't know anything about sports. Michael probably should join Little League or something."

"That would help." He searched her eyes. "You really don't want to marry again?"

Surprised, she shook her head.

"For me, it's different," he said. "I've never been married, but you were once, and from what you've said, I think it was satisfying." He eyed her. "Or am I wrong?"

"No, it was good…most of the time." She faltered over her response, jarred by the truth, but she had promised God for better or worse. "I look at it this way. A man can only add complications to my life." She paused before she admitted the rest. "Complications and fear. I don't want to find myself facing another tragedy that'll throw our lives out of balance again. It took too long to feel alive. I don't think I'm willing to face it again."

"What makes you think you'd have to face a tragedy?"

She glanced through the window. "Look at your dad. Look at you. You're on the brink of a sadness that will change your lives forever. I'm not willing to deal with it again."

Dale drew back and shoved his hands into his pockets without speaking. "Love's not worth the risk?"

"You tell me. I don't see you taking a chance."

A sudden look of surprise shot across his face. "I guess you got me there."

She found her chance to escape and walked to the refrigerator, noticing Kristin's drawing already attached to the door. She opened it and slid in a dish of leftovers. When she turned back, Dale was watching her.

"Michael's seven?" he asked.

She nodded. "Last April. Kristin will be five at the end of the month."

"Five's pretty important. I suppose she wants a party." He turned on the tap and swished a plate beneath the water.

"I don't know for sure, but we'll do something." She carried another stack of dishes to the sink and rinsed them under the tap while Dale added them to the dishwasher.

"I just read in the paper about the Grand Haven Sand Sculpture Contest at the end of June." He turned toward her, still clutching a plate while water dripped to the floor. "Maybe you could take her to the beach to see the sculptures. Michael might enjoy that, too."

"Thanks for the idea," she said, setting another container into the refrigerator. Bev noted he didn't offer to go, but he did make the suggestion. "I'll leave it up to Kristin. She can decide."

He turned off the water and wiped his hands on a towel, then ambled toward her and put his arm around her shoulder. "Good idea. Kids need to learn to make decisions. Then when she's an adult, she can make wise choices. Know what I mean?"

When she looked up, Dale's gaze penetrated hers. He lifted a finger and ran it along the line of her lips. She caught her breath and turned away. She needed to get a grip on herself. Friendship wasn't supposed to feel like this.

Chapter Seven

Bev curled up on the sofa, her eyes aimed at the television while her mind was somewhere else. The house was quiet. The kids had gone to the park with a friend's parent, and Bev had opted to stay home. Sometimes she needed a few minutes to herself.

Today her thinking weighed heavy. Since her serious talk with Dale about being friends, she'd enjoyed his company. He was only around on the weekends, but she found it a wonderful diversion from her usual Saturday of house-cleaning and kid-entertaining.

But since the Memorial Day picnic a week ago, she'd had second thoughts. How could a comfortable friendship agitate her so? Bev let the sensation roll over her again. She'd gone from tolerating Dale to liking him, and now she couldn't get him out of her mind. He caressed her thoughts like satin sheets.

The situation opposed her plans. She'd wanted an easygoing friendship—a companion, not someone who occupied her mind much of the day. Bev hoped it was only the newness of the relationship. Despite her hesitation, she felt a new sense of purpose knowing Dale would be coming for the weekend. He'd plowed into her life and changed it. But how could she be friends when her heart was pulling her in unwanted directions?

While the light from the TV flickered across the room, Bev closed her eyes and sent up a prayer. She needed God's support and strength. She needed to stay firm in her conviction that marriage wasn't for her or for the good of the children. They came first. She really liked Dale and enjoyed his company, but she would never change him. Kids weren't his cup of tea…or coffee either. Friendship was one thing, but when her mind willed itself in a direction beyond she needed help.

A portion of a Bible passage flew to her mind. *The Lord is my strength and my shield.* What was God telling her? She understood the strength part. She needed that, but what about the shield?

As the words wound through her, she felt her heart skip with awareness. God had heard her prayer and sent her the verse to give her a warning. Did she need to protect herself from Dale? She'd already alerted herself to the problem. Whatever the Lord meant, she prayed He would continue to guide her footsteps.

Sounds from outside caught Bev's attention. She rose

and snapped on the porch light as her mother came up the front steps. Bev opened the door to greet her. "You look tired, Mom."

Mildred stepped inside; she was more silent than usual, and Bev knew something was wrong. "This has been a difficult day. Dotty's not doing well, and I stayed for Al."

"What's wrong?"

"An infection. She was running such a high temperature I called the doctor, and we took her to Emergency. They did a catheterization and gave her antibiotics. She's home now, but it's not good."

"I'm so sorry," Bev said, giving her mother a hug.

"While we waited, Al kept repeating over and over that I was the answer to his prayers."

"And you are, Mom. God led you here to Loving for this purpose."

Mildred relaxed her shoulders, made her way to an easy chair and sank into the cushion. "I reminded him of our promise years ago. I know if the tables were turned and Al knew I needed him, he would be there for me."

Bev wasn't sure, but knowing her mother and Al, she wouldn't be surprised. They had the kind of friendship that seemed so rare, a true love and devotion without the romance—the kind of relationship she'd love to have with Dale. Still, Dale's belief that every person only had one soul mate didn't fly when she thought about her mother and Al. They seemed perfect friends. Soul mates.

"Al called Dale and talked with him about Dotty's condition. He was upset, naturally. He said he'd try to take a few days off to spend more time with his mother. I told Al to tell him I'd be there and not to worry, but Dale said he would come anyway."

"She's Dale's mother. It only makes sense he wants to be with her." Bev felt a cold chill settling over her. She prayed her mother would use good sense at the Levins'. Dale and his father needed time alone. She longed to say something, but the right words wouldn't come without hurting her mother's feelings.

"Speaking of Dale, he asked me to go to the boat races on Saturday. Maybe the new problem with Dotty will change that, but if not, will you watch the kids?"

Mildred did a slow turn as if she were in a dream. "Saturday? It depends. Not if Al needs me."

"That's fine. If he does, I'll get a baby-sitter." She studied her mother for a moment and took a chance on speaking her mind. "You can't be there every minute of the day. When Al's home or Dale's there, you can give them a chance to spend some time alone with Dotty."

"Do you think I'm interfering? I'm a nurse, Bev. I'm not meddling in their lives."

"I didn't suggest you were. I only meant you might want to be sensitive to their needs." Dale's needs were her real concern.

"I'm a professional. I have good sense, Bev."

"I know, Mom."

But did she? Her mother had already been spending all day and into the evening at the Levins' without being the official caregiver. What would happen when she was?

Dale glanced at Bev, then back at the traffic. He'd never seen her so stressed.

"The evening started off badly," he said, knowing she'd had a difficult time with the kids.

"Can you imagine hearing your daughter scream 'I hate you?'"

Dale couldn't imagine having a daughter, period.

Bev lifted her fingers and massaged the center of her forehead.

"Headache?"

She gave him a fleeting nod. "I feel like a rubber band being pulled in every direction. I'm ready to snap."

"You're a frustrated mother." He placed his arm around her shoulders. "You know psychology. Kids want attention. If they don't get attention for being good, they get it for being bad. That's what happened today."

"Never mind. It's my problem."

"Not anymore. It's the baby-sitter's." Dale reached across the seat and brushed his palm along Bev's arm. "The kids wanted your attention tonight. You were leaving without them. You rarely do that. So they didn't know how else to get your attention except by using the way that they know best."

She grimaced. "And they got what they wanted."

"Only in part." He hated to see her so frustrated. Parenthood wasn't for him, especially if it were like this all the time. He left his hand resting against her arm, moving it in slow circles and hoping she understood he cared. "The kids got your attention, but it didn't work. They wanted you to stay home, but you didn't. That's a mark in your favor."

"I don't know why I let them rile me," Bev said. "I go off like I don't have a brain in my head."

"You're frustrated."

"What would you do?" she asked.

"Let them make decisions. Give them options—but you pick the choices. You're a child-care worker. Treat your kids like you do the ones at Loving Care."

She stared at him as if she'd never realized the connection. "It's easier there."

"Because you have nothing vested. You care about the kids, but they're not your flesh and blood. That changes everything." And how well he knew that.

Dale wanted to beat his head against a wall for letting Bev get under his skin. A woman with kids. He knew better. Talk about making choices. He'd let his heart make the choices and not his head.

"I use choice options at work," he said. "It's a tremendous way to let people think they're deciding when you've set up the limits."

She nodded. "Give me an example."

Dale scrambled for an idea. What did he know about

kids? "Okay." His mind grasped at choices. "Here goes. 'Michael, you can watch TV for a half hour, or you can play the game with your sister and then watch TV until bedtime. You decide.'"

Bev's face brightened. "I suppose I do give limited choices at the day care."

They drove a block before Bev broke the silence. "I thought you didn't know anything about kids."

He glanced at her, then back to the traffic. "I don't. I'm using common sense. I'm no authority, Bev. I'm just tossing out possibilities to help you. I suppose I should keep my mouth shut." How many times had she told him to stay out of her business?

She tugged at her seat belt so she could shift to face him. "No, don't. Sometimes I get irked when you butt in, but I'm getting to know you better. You're trying to help."

Help. He'd needed that himself for a long time. He still did. "I am. Friends help friends, Bev. You've given me food for thought more than once. I've even picked up my Bible a few times."

"But did you open it?" A faint grin joined her hopeful expression.

"I have. Even read some passages."

She nodded, her face looking more content than he'd seen it since she'd climbed into his car.

Dale turned his attention to the highway, but his thoughts lingered on Bev. His heart went out to her—

raising two kids alone, learning to live without a marriage partner and adjusting to a new job. Even one major life change was hard to handle. Thinking of his mother's illness, Dale could relate.

A partner. That's one thing he missed staying single. Someone special to share his time and thoughts. He had buddies, but that was different. Men talked sports and cars. They discussed politics and the latest TV programs, but they didn't talk about what was in their gut. Never. But with a woman, he could talk about how deeply he worried about his parents and how much he enjoyed a sunset.

He gazed into the bright summer sky and yearned for something he couldn't put his finger on. Lately, Dale had realized he didn't have much to make his life worthwhile. He did his job well. He loved his parents and honored them, but besides that, he hadn't made a mark on the world. If he died tomorrow, he'd be forgotten once his folks were gone.

People with children left something important behind. Another human. A whole lineage of people. Look at Sarah and Abraham. He thought of the biblical "begats" that he'd always found so boring when he'd read the Bible years ago, but now that he thought about it, maybe the Lord was saying something to humankind. When we create a life, we leave our mark on the world.

Bev would leave her mark with two children.

Though kids could be frustrating, he'd watched Bev's face light up in those moments when the kids were thoughtful or fun. He couldn't imagine having a child of his own, part of him that would continue after he was gone.

He halted his thoughts and turned down Howard Street to Harbor Drive. When he came to the harbourfront parking lot, he pulled in.

"This is it," he said. "They'll sail along here into the marina."

Bev collected her handbag and sweater while he climbed out and rounded the car to meet her. When he opened the door, she sent him a smile that warmed him more than a summer heat wave. When she stepped onto the concrete, Dale took her arm and guided her across the street to the Lake Michigan shoreline.

They followed the boardwalk and settled on the large set of bleachers used for waterfront events. Today it was filled with people waiting for the racers.

Off in the distance, a few sails jutted above the horizon. Dale pointed toward them as they heaved forward on the billowing turquoise water. The sun lowered in the sky, dipping into the endless lake and sending its golden fingers flickering across the waves.

The boats reminded Dale of himself, tossing around on an endless sea of waves, heading for a distant shore he had yet to know. Frightening. Lately, between his mother's problems and Bev stepping into his life, he'd felt lost. She'd thrown off his plans and filled his mind, but in his heart, he sensed he could never make a commitment or say "I love you."

A breeze blew, and he felt Bev shudder with the cooler temperature. He slipped his arm around her shoulder. "Is that better?" he asked.

She smiled and snuggled closer.

Dale tucked her against him as his thoughts wandered away to forbidden realms. If he were smart, he'd take back his arm and control the forces that swelled within him. But the sweet sensation won out, and he let himself enjoy the moment.

Bev's hair ruffled with the breeze and tresses brushed against Dale's face, arousing his senses and leaving him thoughtful. He knew so little about her. How had widowhood impacted her? Had her marriage been a good one? Had her husband been her soul mate? If he were correct, the man had to be the one God wanted her to be with forever, bound by an oath of love.

"This is wonderful," Bev said. "I can't believe I've lived here most of my life and never seen the races."

He saw a flicker of sadness in her eyes that piqued his interest.

"Tell me about yourself, Bev." He tilted her chin toward his face. "Remember? Today's my turn."

She gave him a halfhearted grin, but he knew it was a cover-up. He'd gotten to know Bev well enough to recognize the nuances in her face.

"Nothing exciting," she said, turning her attention toward the sailboats.

He wanted to look in her eyes, but she resisted and he didn't persist.

"I was born in Loving. When I was in high school my father was transferred to the Detroit area. I was miserable leaving all my friends."

"You graduated in Detroit?"

"Warren, Michigan, actually. Then I went to junior college. I didn't know what I wanted to be, but college seemed the thing to do. I met Jesse there. We'd known each other in Loving, although we hadn't been close then. We married and moved back here. That's about it."

But Dale knew that wasn't all of it.

Bev's hazel eyes darkened when she finally looked at him. "Jesse died three years ago in a motorcycling accident. I'd stopped working to raise the kids. I had a hard time."

"With two kids, I can imagine."

"Kristin was only one. She doesn't remember Jesse, but Michael has a few memories. His father really doted on him."

The image rose in Dale's thoughts like a shadow, and he sensed the impact his father's death had made on Michael. Now, as an adult, Dale was facing a similar grief of his own. "What did you do after Jesse died?"

She lowered her gaze again. "Jesse left no insurance. I had no income and too much pride for assistance, so

I did what mothers do. I found a job at Loving Care." She lifted her head, her face brighter. "It's actually been a great experience. I could take the kids with me. After Michael started school, I only had Kristin, and next September, she'll enter kindergarten."

Dale wanted to ask why Jesse had had no insurance and exactly how he had died, but he could see Bev's discomfort and swallowed the questions. All he could do was hug Bev even closer to his side. He knew her life had been difficult and felt he'd added to her problems with his attitude toward her kids. He needed to try harder to be a good friend and not a selective one.

An opportunity came to mind. Dale loved Bev's company, and he figured he could deal with the children occasionally. "Any decisions about Kristin's birthday?"

"Yes. She's excited about the sand sculpture so that'll be a nice day for her."

"Would you like me to come along? We could have a picnic on the beach."

She lifted her head and gave him a questioning gaze. "Are you serious?"

Was he? The question flew through his mind, but he answered with a quick, "Sure."

"That would be nice."

Dale's thoughts scattered through his head. Friends did things for friends. Millie's devotion to his father came to mind, but the reference also sent a charge of irritation through Dale. He had little time alone with his mother anymore since Millie was huddling over her. When he tried to do something, Millie took over. He wanted to help his mother. He owed her that, but getting around Millie seemed impossible. She'd taken over their home.

Dale dismissed his thoughts. Why ruin a pleasant day? Instead he looked across the water at the sailboats that now neared the shore, their hulls digging into the rolling surf. Dale's emotions pitched and tossed, leaving him as confounded as the sailboats' wild ride.

His only hope was to find an anchor—to moor his emotions before he drowned.

Chapter Eight

Dale pulled the picnic hamper out of his trunk while Bev helped the kids climb from the car. A soft breeze ruffled Dale's shirt as he hoisted the basket onto his arm. He looked toward the Lake Michigan beach; the bright June sun shimmered off the sand and the indigo water washed to shore with a billowing swish. If only life could be so perfect.

He liked Bev—a lot, if he were truthful—and if he wanted to spend time with her, he needed to tolerate the children and enjoy Kristin's birthday.

"Beautiful day," Bev said, circling the car. She extended her arms. "Let me help."

He handed her the picnic basket, pulled out the cooler and called over his shoulder, "Can you kids handle these sand chairs?"

Before the last words left his mouth, the children

had vanished, scurrying toward the picnic tables. Dale clamped his mouth closed to avoid making a comment or bellowing at them. No sense riling Bev and ruining the pleasant day.

Bev went on ahead, leaving Dale behind to balance the chairs on the cooler so he could carry them. As he followed, he calmed himself and admired Bev's shapely form. She'd worn white shorts with a blue-striped knit top and had wound her hair into a knot. The wind played among the clasps, pulling strands loose as she headed for the picnic tables.

While Dale struggled along doing a balancing act, his gaze shifted to the Grand Haven pier jutting far into the lake. The old and new lighthouses stood at its end like red sentinels guarding the shoreline.

The children noticed the lights and pointed. Kristin twirled in the sand, excitement evident on her face, while Michael ran on ahead.

"The lighthouses," Bev called. "They want to go up there."

"Before we eat?" he asked, finally catching up to her.

The kids' sweatshirts lay discarded beside the picnic table while they stood in the distance beckoning and waving as they jigged in the sand.

Dale unloaded the gear, then joined Bev as she headed for the pier. He caught her hand and pulled her forward while her laughter rang in his ears along with the pounding of the surf against the breakwater.

"Be careful," Dale called to the children. "The pier is slippery."

The kids held back, and Dale was pleased to see Michael mind for once.

"Thank you," he said when he reached them. He gave Kristin's ponytail a playful tug. "We have to be careful."

Kristin wrinkled her nose and grinned.

Bev looked relaxed as they walked the wide weather-worn planks. The kids scurried down the middle, then ran back, staying close to their sides.

Contentment engulfed him, away from the stress of work and his mother's illness. Though Millie irked him at times, Dale saw a difference in his father's face; he looked more relaxed, and he smiled so much more than he had. Something about Bev's family lifted people's spirits. Often he found himself grinning like the Cheshire cat at Bev.

Dale tucked his hands into his pockets and looked down between the planks to the roiling surf. When Bev stopped along the rail, Dale joined her, watching the surf roll in, smashing against the pilings in a gigantic spray. "I'm sure this will be a special birthday for Kristin," Bev said. "Thanks for suggesting it."

"You're welcome." Dale's thoughts segued from Kristin's birthday to his mother's—possibly her last. It was coming up soon, and sorrow spiraled through him. He wanted to do something special for her, too.

The children called to them, and he and Bev turned

away from the railing. When they reached the children, Michael was sitting on the lighthouse's entrance steps. "Can we go inside?"

"It's locked," Dale said. "They don't use this lighthouse anymore."

Michael rose and tried the door again, yanking on the handle with all his strength.

"Who turns on the light?" Kristin asked, looking up toward the glass dome at the top.

"The U.S. Coast Guard lights the new one at the end of the pier," Dale said. "They're stationed in Grand Haven."

She wrinkled her nose. "Are they the water police?"

Dale choked back a chuckle. "I suppose you could say that," he said. "They're a branch of the military. You know what that is?"

"Army guys," Michael said.

Dale smiled. "Sort of." He turned to Bev with a whisper. "But don't let them hear anyone call them that." He couldn't help but chuckle at the kid's curiosity.

Bored with the door that wouldn't open, Michael moved ahead with Kristin on his heels, heading for the pier's end where the new, squatty building now served as the harbor's beacon. Dale and Bev followed behind, keeping their eyes on the children.

"I don't understand you," Bev said.

Her comment brought Dale to attention. "Don't understand what?"

"Why you agreed to come today, and why you're so natural with the kids. You've taken the time to answer their questions, and you've really been nice." An embarrassed expression swept across her face. "I mean you're nice, but you're not usually relaxed with them."

Dale hadn't come along to be with the kids. He'd come to be with her—to impress her, really—but how could he tell her that? Dale shrugged. "Kids are kids. They're curious. I answered their questions."

Her expression indicated she figured there was more to it, but she didn't press the issue. Instead she changed the subject. "Why haven't you married, Dale? Is it because of kids?"

Her blunt question struck him like a bullwhip, coiling around him with a sting. What could he say that wouldn't offend her? He grasped at the only thing he could. The truth.

"It's not kids. Not totally, and I've already told you. I believe in 'until death us do part.' I don't want to make a mistake, and my parents' marriage has been a model for me. I don't know if I have it in me to make that kind of self-sacrificing commitment for a marriage or for children."

Bev's curiosity sank to disappointment. "I can't believe that. I remember you talking about people having one soul mate, but it's got to be something deeper than that. You have such a capacity to love. I see it in your relationship with your parents. You have so much to offer. I just don't understand."

He gave up and realized he had to be honest. "It's fear."

"Fear?"

"Love turns friendship into a right arm."

Bev frowned. "What does that mean?"

"I can live without a friend. But I can't bear the thought of losing my right arm. Life changes. I would experience a loss that's incomprehensible. My mother is a perfect example. If I never love, I'll never feel grief again."

Bev let out a lengthy sigh that rose above the din of wind and water. "Dale, I can't believe you're saying this. You'd rather be without love to avoid sorrow."

"They're inseparable, aren't they? Love and sorrow. They go hand in hand."

Her face twisted with dismay. "Please, don't say that. Look at my mother. She loved my dad with all her heart. She's smiling again. Her life has purpose. I lost a husband, but I'm smiling again. I have a meaningful life."

"Smiling, maybe, but you're not married now either. Why not?" She seemed to crumple at his question, as if today was the first time she'd seen the similarity. "Don't tell me no one has shown interest in you. I won't believe it."

"Well, you can believe it, Dale. I've never dated. My kids have been my life since Jesse died. I know three years is a long time, but to be honest, life's almost easier now. I only have two people to worry about, and they have to listen to me—at least most of the time. Jesse didn't or he wouldn't be dead."

Her voice carried such emotion that Dale wished he could roll back the clock and delete what had just happened. "I'm sorry, Bev. I'm not trying to drag up your past. I was just trying to make a comparison."

Her eyes looked misted, and he didn't know if it was from the memories of her husband or his comments about love and marriage. He grasped her arm and slowed her to a stop. She avoided looking into his face, and he touched his fingers to her chin and eased her to focus on him. "Let's change the subject, okay? It's a lovely day, the kids are having fun and we have a picnic to eat. I don't want to add tension to what's been a tremendous day."

Though her eyes were facing him, he saw she wasn't giving him a direct look, but she gave him a single nod. "You're right." She finally focused and sent him the flicker of a smile. "Some other time."

"Some other time," he agreed. He wrapped his arm around her and drew her closer. "We both have things to think about."

She tilted her face upward, and this time her smile seemed warmer and more sincere.

Surprising himself, he bent and kissed her temple.

Bev didn't pull away, but raised her hand and pressed it against his cheek. The feeling rolled through him like a tidal wave, and he struggled to keep himself from kissing her mouth.

When Dale turned his eyes from Bev, he noticed the children had reached the end of the pier. They came bounding back toward them, eager to start back. Both moaned that they wanted to eat their lunch and see the sand sculptures.

Dale and Bev turned back while the kids scurried on ahead, but Michael decided to make it a race. Before anyone could stop them, Kristin let out a screaming protest as Michael set off, passing her in a heartbeat.

Fearing the slippery, uneven pier, Dale dashed off after Michael with Bev trying to keep up with him.

"Michael," Bev called. Her voice was lost in the pounding of the waves against the pier's foundation pillars.

Michael remained in the lead, the shoestrings of one of his sneakers whipping around his ankles as he ran. Fear struck Dale, but he'd noticed the laces too late. "Michael," he yelled, not caring whether Bev was angry at him.

Michael didn't hear or heed Dale's call. He glanced over his shoulder and barreled ahead. As Dale watched, the boy stepped on a lace and toppled forward, stumbling along the pier toward the railing.

Dale shot forward like a dart, a prayer—his first in years—rising to heaven. As Michael skidded along the edge, Dale reached toward the boy and clutched

Michael's arm, jerking him to a sudden stop. Without thinking, Dale drew the boy into his arms, feeling tears push behind his eyes. "Why don't you listen?" he yelled. "You could have been killed." He'd never forgive himself if the boy had gone over. Not only was the lake deep, but cables and concrete pilings were hidden beneath the water.

Michael seemed to understand. He clung to Dale until Bev reached his side.

Fear had frozen on her face, and she pulled Michael into her arms in a tight hug. "You scared me to death," she whispered into his ear.

"I didn't mean to," Michael said, as if afraid of being punished.

"I asked you to be careful," Dale said. "I just thank the Lord you're okay."

Michael eased back and gave Dale a downcast nod. He knew he'd not listened earlier, and Dale hoped he'd learned a serious lesson. Before the boy took another step, Bev tied his shoelace into a double knot.

Once the shoe was tied, they all joined hands and walked—slowly this time—until they reached the end of the pier and stepped into the sand.

The children dug into the spread of food Bev had brought along, and after their picnic, Dale guided them down toward the water where they could view the amazing sand sculptures. Although excited about the sand castles, forts and abstract designs, the kids were enthralled at a mermaid created high on the beach away from the waves that surged to shore.

When they tired, they returned to the picnic table. The children carried water from the lake in soda cans to the sand nearby and created their own sculptures. Though they crumbled and toppled as they worked, the activity occupied them while Dale enjoyed the quiet moments with Bev.

He had accepted that he and Bev were friends, and each minute together had been important to him. She was a bright spot in his stressful life. "I'm having a great time today, but I'm also feeling guilt."

"Why?"

"I should have spent the time with my mom and dad."

She dragged the toe of her sneaker through the sandy soil. "I think they understand."

"They do, but I don't. I'm thinking about taking a leave and coming back home for a while." He was surprised he'd blurted his thread of an idea.

"A leave?" Bev shielded the sun from her eyes and gazed at him. "Why now?"

"Because I—I sense the time is getting close. I'm in Grand Rapids and I spend my time worrying about my parents. I have so many things to settle, so much to say, and I'm afraid—"

"I'm not sure that's wise. Your mom just went through the infection scare. I really think your taking a leave will make her think you know something she doesn't. Anyway, now that my mother's taken over it's made your dad's days easier."

Her comment struck him with unexpected force. Her mother had taken over, and maybe that was part of his discomfort, but how could he tell her how irritated he'd become with Millie?

"My mom will tell you when she sees the signs that the time's getting close," Bev said. "She'll be honest."

Dale didn't fear that. Millie would tell them, but Bev had made a good point about making his mother suspect. Dale wanted to do nothing that would make his mother give up hope. "I'm going to take a couple of vacation days for my mom's birthday. It's on a Thursday, and I want to take her somewhere special."

"She'd like having you home for a long weekend." She paused. "So would I."

Her comment surprised him and pleased him. He realized he felt the same, afraid to commit, afraid to love, but he felt so drawn, so attached to Bev.

Dale brushed a sprinkle of sand from Bev's cheek and let his fingers linger over her warm and soft skin. He surprised himself with the unexpected feelings that ran through him. The last thing he wanted to do was hurt her. He'd even startled himself today with the way he felt about Michael. After he'd wanted to give him a swift kick in the pants, he'd found himself thinking of the boy and wondering why he seemed to have one foot in trouble most of the time.

Dale had decided his feelings for Bev and her family had to be a form of empathy. As he faced his mother's death, he could only imagine how their lives had changed when they'd lost a father and a husband. Bev's life had crumbled into dust, and she'd had to rebuild it into something functional, almost like the children trying to create the sand sculptures. One wrong move and everything fell apart.

The same thought fitted his reasons for staying single. Yet, as the thought left his mind, he knew he'd been wrong. Losing his mother, losing a friend or seeing someone else's pain still hurt. He couldn't escape it no matter what he did. Sadness followed joy.

"Why are you so quiet?" Bev brushed sand from his pant leg. "Is something wrong?"

"Just thinking about life. Sometimes it seems so hopeless. So dark."

"Only for nonbelievers, Dale. Remember what the Lord promised. 'Weeping may endure for the night, but joy comes in the morning.'" She brushed her finger along his arm. "You have to be patient. Sorrow fades, and happiness returns. I survived my husband's death. Your dad will survive. You'll survive."

The inevitable rose in his mind, and the thought of being alone overwhelmed him.

Chapter Nine

Bev parked in front of Annie Dewitt's home and headed up the walk. The old-fashioned porch swing hanging from thick chains stirred in the summer breeze and looked inviting. She could imagine sitting there on a warm summer evening.

Annie had asked her to drop by that evening. The visit seemed to have no particular purpose, but Bev wondered. Annie had been quiet at work during the day, and an uneasy feeling washed over her as she approached the door.

For so long Bev had done little without dragging the kids along, but now her mother often baby-sat, even taking the children to Dotty's. As ill as she was, Dotty always asked about the children. They seemed to give her spirit a lift.

Bev rang the bell, and Annie opened the door, a

strained smile on her face. Bev's chest tightened; her uneasiness was justified.

"Hi," Annie said, pushing the door wider. "I'm glad you could come."

As Bev came through the doorway, Gracelynne toddled toward her on chubby legs. "Hello," Bev said, bending down to give the child a hug.

The toddler uttered a lengthy sentence of chatter and waved her soft-covered book at Bev.

"We're not reading books now, sweetie." Annie hoisted the child into her arms and motioned toward the living-room sofa. "Have a seat. I made some tea if you'd like."

"That would be nice," Bev said. She sat with Gracelynne on her lap and played with her while Annie went for the beverage. The child's laughter filled Bev with delight, and she was struck again by how much she loved young children.

Time had flown. Michael was going into second grade, and Kristin would start kindergarten this year. She would have no more babies in her life. At age thirty-four, she knew the time was coming when childbearing would not be wise, and the thought settled in her chest like a knot. Would she ever have another child? It seemed impossible.

Annie returned, and the conversation revolved around Loving Care Child Care, Dotty Levin and Gracelynne.

"She's such a blessing," Annie said. "When we adopted her, she was the answer to our prayers. I was too old to have a child…I thought, and—"

Her face paled, and Bev searched her strained expression for the reason. "Annie? Is something wrong?"

Annie's chin lifted in surprise. "What do you mean?"

"You're not yourself today. You have something on your mind."

Annie didn't speak but lowered her head.

Bev caught the moisture brimming in Annie's eyes. "Please, tell me. Are you and Ken having problems?" Concern rifled through her with the question.

"No. Ken and I are very happy. He's a wonderful husband."

"Is it Gracelynne?" The child looked the picture of health, but Annie's stress signaled something was very wrong.

"I'm pregnant," Annie said.

"Pregnant?" The admission raced through Bev and left her with an unexpected feeling of envy. She remembered vividly the joy of having a new baby cuddled against her.

Annie nodded. "We were as shocked as you are. I'm too old, and I don't know what to do."

"Apparently you're not too old," Bev said.

"I'm forty-four."

Bev's earlier thoughts sprung to mind. She was ten years younger than Annie and had decided she was too old. But now…

"People have babies at your age," Bev said. "Women in their fifties have children."

"Not me," Annie said. "Impossible."

"Obviously, not impossible." She tried to sound lighthearted for Annie.

"We just didn't think it would happen. I'm really afraid, Bev. The baby will be in danger. I don't care about myself, but—"

"You can't discredit the Lord's gift, Annie. He's chosen you to be the mother of your own biological child."

"But it's not wise. I really think we need to…" her voice faded "…make decisions."

"The Lord's made the decision. You have no decision to make. You're having a baby."

Tears rolled down Annie's cheeks. "I'm ashamed of myself. I know I'll have the baby. I'm just so frightened."

"You'll need to take good care of yourself and follow the doctor's orders. There's no reason why you can't have a healthy baby."

Annie brushed the tears away with the back of her hand.

Bev crossed to her side and sat on the chair arm. She wrapped her arm around Annie's shoulder. "The Lord gives us nothing that we can't handle." Her words nudged her own concerns, and she recalled how poorly she'd handled so many of the stresses in her life.

Annie tilted her head and gave a faint nod. "Despite my fear, I think Ken's thrilled. I should be, too. We'd been talking about adopting another child, but then we just let the idea pass."

"God did it for you. You're a wonderful mother to Gracelynne, Annie, and Ken's a doting father. This new baby will be very blessed."

"Thank you," Annie whispered. "I'm ashamed of myself for even doubting."

"Annie, we all doubt. We all question God's plan for us. He knows our weaknesses, and He forgives us."

"Thanks for reminding me." She gave Bev a faint smile. "It feels so good to talk with someone."

"It's nice, isn't it?" Bev said. "I always have lots of thoughts going through my mind—things I don't want to share with my mom, but things I'd like to talk about."

"Talk away," Annie said. "It's good to know I'm not the only one who needs counseling."

Bev looked at her and didn't know what to say or where to begin. "It struck me again today when I saw Gracelynne. I've watched my two kids grow, and I've thought for so long I was done having children. Then out of the blue, I feel heartbroken to think I'll never have another child. My arms ache to hold a newborn baby—one that's my own—but babies mean marriage, and I'm afraid. I don't want to go through it again. Once was enough."

"What about you and Dale? I thought your relationship looked promising."

Bev shrugged. "No. Dale's been very open about not looking for marriage. He enjoys the friendship. With his mom's illness, he needs someone to talk with, too, and I'm the one. I truly think that's where it will end."

Annie frowned. "Are you sure? I see much more going on than you do."

"What do you mean?"

"I've seen the way he looks at you. Don't give up on that relationship. Let God's will be done."

"I try, but I'm not very good at it."

Annie laughed. "None of us are."

"Like I said, once is enough, and yet—" She paused, unable to face the new feelings. "My thoughts waver. I'm not certain I want a commitment. My life feels settled, and for once I'm in control. I'm not spending hours worrying about a partner who willingly endangers his life without thinking of his family. I'd rather be alone."

Annie pressed her warm hand against Bev's arm. "I was alone for many years, Bev. It's not good. I tolerated it. A life shared with someone special is what God wants for us, I think. The Bible says that man shouldn't be alone." She sent Bev a feeble grin. "I think that means women, too."

Bev slid her hand over Annie's. "I don't know, Annie. Maybe you're right, but I need to be certain and know what I'm feeling is real." She thought a moment. "Could we pray? I think we both need God to give us strength and understanding of what he wants for us."

"I'd love to pray with you," Annie said.

As if she understood, Gracelynne teetered toward them and pressed her tiny hands against theirs and gurgled one of her cryptic monologues.

Annie shot Bev a gentle smile. "From the mouths of babes."

"They touch our lives and hearts," Bev said, as they bowed their heads.

Bev followed her mother into the church. The strains of music rose above the sounds of worshippers greeting each other as they settled into the pews. As they made their way down the aisle, Mildred came to an abrupt halt, and Bev ran into her from behind.

"Sorry," Bev said, wondering why her mother had halted.

"There's Al and Dale," Millie said, waving her hand toward them.

Bev faltered, hoping they would sit somewhere else. If Annie thought she and Dale were forming a relationship, sitting with him would have the whole congregation thinking the same. She couldn't stop her mother, however. Mildred had bustled ahead and was already seated by the time Bev reached her.

They whispered good mornings, and before the service began, Michael appeared at her side.

"What's wrong?" Bev asked.

"I don't want to go to Sunday school today."

"Why not?" Bev studied his face and noticed his gaze was glued to Dale.

"Can I stay in church?"

Michael was more difficult to dissuade than her

mother, and she shifted over for him to take a seat. She was pleased, at least, that Kristin hadn't followed him.

He sank beside her a moment, then moved around to sit between her and Mildred. Before she realized, Michael had made his way along the line until he finally wriggled in beside Dale. She watched Dale's face and caught his puzzled look.

Concern washed over her. Michael was becoming too attached to Dale. He talked about him constantly. One day Dale would walk away and settle back into his life in Grand Rapids. Michael would be forgotten, and Bev would once again be left with a boy abandoned by the only male figure in his life. She didn't know how to avoid the boy's inevitable heartbreak.

Bev had to admit that Michael had changed. He wasn't perfect, but he'd calmed down, and his need for attention had faded a little. He and Kristin even seemed to get along better.

The worship music swelled, and the congregation rose. Bev followed their lead from habit while her mind struggled with the negatives and positives of her relationship with Dale. Confused and getting nowhere, she pushed the thoughts aside.

The hymn ended, and Bev sank into her seat and opened the pew Bible to follow the pastor's reading from Romans 15. The words marched through her until the last phrase washed over her like a benediction. "May the God of hope fill you with all joy and peace as you trust in Him, so that you may overflow with hope by the power of the Holy Spirit."

Trust in Him. No matter how hard Bev tried, she knew she hadn't trusted in the Lord the way He had asked of her. God's promise was filled with all she needed—joy, peace and hope overflowing. *Hope.* A single word that held such assurance. If only she could grasp it and hold it in her heart.

Voices rose around her, and she opened her hymn book and joined in the song. "Blessed assurance, Jesus is mine." As the words left her, her eyes drifted to Michael so close to Dale, his gaze enrapt on the man's face.

Her eyes shifted to Al, his bass voice booming, and her mother, standing beside him, using his songbook to sing. They looked like a happy family when they weren't that at all. They were people struggling with private matters, needing the wonderful assurance that God was in charge.

When the service ended, she shifted into the aisle, and Dale joined her as they headed outside. The bright sun warmed her, and the pleasant day gave her courage to be open with him.

"I'm concerned about Michael," Bev said.

He frowned. "You mean missing Sunday school?"

"No. You. Hero worship," Bev said. "I don't think it's good for him."

"I suppose it's the need for attention we talked about a while back."

Mildred joined them, rattling on about someone Bev didn't know, and she let her thoughts weigh what Dale had said. It might be attention, but her heart asked if Michael would be okay. What would happen when—

Michael suddenly appeared at Dale's side while Al's voice cut through Bev's thoughts. "Dale, you ought to take this young man to the baseball game. He'd like that." He tousled Michael's hair. "And if Millie stays with your mother, I'll go along with you."

Michael's eyes widened and Bev saw the excitement grow on his face.

"I'd be glad to," Mildred said, her gaze shifting from Al to Dale's bewildered expression.

"Baseball game?" Dale asked, looking as if he'd rather scrub floors.

"The youth group," Al said. "You'd like that, wouldn't you, Michael?"

Michael's head bobbed like a buoy on rough water.

"Well, I…" Dale looked from his father to Bev to Michael. The boy's eager face tilted upward to Dale's as if he were the sun.

Bev watched Dale crumple with defeat. He glanced at his watch. "When does it start?"

"The bulletin said right after church. We might have time to pick up a burger."

Mildred bustled into the conversation. "What about Kristin?"

"I doubt if she'd enjoy a ball game," Dale said.

"It's just for boys," Michael added, his tone filled with importance.

Dale gave Bev a look. "It'll be good for him to do something without—" He gave a toss of his head toward Kristin who came bounding toward them.

The situation felt uncomfortable to Bev. She knew Al had roped Dale into the situation. He didn't want to take Michael, but she knew she'd let Michael go despite her reservations. Michael needed a male role model, and Dale and his father were as good as any. Yet that frustrated her, too. How could she dislike and like something at the same time? She knew the answer. Dale's attention and Michael's eager acceptance made Bev feel inadequate. She needed to deal with her own sense of insecurity.

Kristin flashed a construction-paper creation toward her. "It's for you, Mama."

Bev only half looked as she watched Michael skip off with Dale and Al.

"You didn't look," Kristin whined. Mildred gazed at the picture, complimenting Kristin's handiwork.

Finally Bev pulled her gaze away from the men and studied the jagged circle she guessed was the world arched by a rainbow. "It's beautiful, Kristin."

"It's for you. It's God's promise," Kristin said, pointing to the colorful semicircle.

God's promise. The words took her back to the worship service. Hope and blessed assurance. Bev hugged the Sunday-school project against her chest. "I love this," she said, bending down to kiss her daughter's cheek. "Thank you."

When she lifted her gaze, Dale and Michael were at the far end of the parking lot. Michael saw her watching and waved.

Her chest tightened. Was all of this God's doing? A single word rose in her thoughts.

Trust.

Chapter Ten

Bev pulled into the parking lot of Loving Treasures boutique. Dale had planned an outing to the Star-Spangled Butterfly Festival for Dotty's birthday, and if she was going, she wanted to take along a gift. But what? She had a difficult time thinking of something appropriate for a woman who was so ill.

Her gaze drifted to the lake and the flurry of tourists who filled the streets. Yesterday had been the Fourth of July. She'd spent a quiet holiday—a disappointingly quiet day.

She'd assumed Dale's family would plan a picnic or attend the Grand Haven fireworks, but Dotty hadn't been up to it, so Bev had had nothing to do. Even Dale had stayed in Grand Rapids to catch up on work. While her mother spent the day with Dotty and Al, Bev had stayed home with the children. She took them to the fireworks by herself.

Bev disliked the empty feeling she had when Dale wasn't around. She'd warned herself not to open herself to a man, but she hadn't listened.

Nothing made sense anymore, and Bev knew she depended on the Levins too much. But what could she do now? The feeling of family and their friendship had turned her and the children's life into something warm and comforting.

Looking into the front window of Loving Treasures, Bev perused the display. Handbags made no sense for Dotty. Evening shawls, flowery umbrellas, costume jewelry—she let the items filter through her mind. She figured Claire would have some ideas and pushed open the door.

A bell tinkled above the door, and as she stepped inside, Claire came sweeping from the back room. Though the woman toned down her garb at church, today she appeared to have stepped out of a Hawaiian movie. Wrapped in a tropical-print muumuu, she had a hibiscus pinned in her long, flowing red hair.

"How nice to see you," Claire said, gliding silently across the floor.

Bev sent her a smile, wondering if Claire was barefoot to capture the mood of her wardrobe. Peeking down to the floor, she glimpsed at ballet slippers. "I need a birthday gift for Mrs. Levin," Bev said.

"Hmm?" Claire pinched her bright-orange lips and raised her gaze toward the ceiling. "She doesn't get out much, I know."

"Rarely. Sometimes into the backyard and this week Dale's taking her to the butterfly festival at Hoffmaster Park."

"Butterflies." Claire's voice lifted with the word. She spun around and sailed toward a display counter. She fluttered through a stack of colorful scarves until she found what she had in mind. Like a magician, she tugged the silk cloth from the pile in a dramatic sweep and waved it in the air. As it settled on the counter, Bev could see the butterfly design in brilliant shades of blue, orange, sienna and red.

"Perfect," Claire said. "A lovely scarf to wear encapsulating the memory of the special day."

Bev studied the bright fabric and agreed it was both practical and frivolous. "I like it, and I think Dotty will, too."

Claire's face glowed as she carried the scarf to the register, wrapped it in tissue and slid it into a bag. "You make such a wonderful family. It's so nice to see you all together in church."

"We're not exactly a family," Bev said. She knew she'd better stop any speculation before the idea traveled and caused someone grief. "My mom works for the Levins."

"Yes, but I can see the love you all share. Your little boy's latched on to Dale Levin like a father figure. I'm sure you've noticed."

Bev squirmed with her comment. Once Dotty... She let the word fade in her thoughts. Death wasn't something she wanted to think about now. She'd recently returned to the land of the living, and she had no desire to spend her time wallowing in grief again.

Bev managed a smile. "You know children. They take advantage of anyone who shows them attention."

Claire eyed her as if she had something to say but realized she'd make no progress saying it.

Bev opened her wallet and handed Claire some bills, curious as to what the woman had on her mind.

Claire made change and laid it into Bev's palm. "There you go." She closed the register drawer and stepped from behind the counter. "I'm sure Dotty will be pleased with the scarf. It's such a shame she's deteriorated so quickly. I know it's hard on Al." She adjusted one of her long colorful earrings. "I enjoy seeing him smile again. Your mother has turned his life around. Before she came, Al broke my heart."

"Mom and Al are old high-school friends," Bev said, concerned that Claire was reading something into the relationship.

"Yes, I know. Old friends are a special breed."

Bev gestured to the package. "Thanks for the gift idea, Claire." She backed toward the door, her mind heavy with their conversation.

"Come back again. I can always come up with something that makes a lovely gift."

"I know you can," Bev said. She opened the door and stepped outside, drawing in the warm, lake-scented air.

She could hear the bell tinkle behind the glass as she closed the door. Her steps were hurried as she headed for the car. Bev wondered if she should caution her mother that her closeness with Al might breed speculation.

Bev's parents had been very close and always loving. Bev's marriage hadn't been at all like her parents'. It had seemed wrought with stress. Now her mother had stepped into another loving relationship with Al and Dotty. They adored her, and her life was full. Bev's relationship with Dale seemed thwarted with problems and tension. Why?

It didn't seem fair.

But then, no one said life was fair.

The warm July sun shimmered from the concrete sidewalks as they made their way through Hoffmaster Park. Dotty had loved the butterfly-print scarf when she'd opened the gift. She wound it around her neck, and the colors brightened her face. Today she looked more healthy than she had the last few times Bev had seen her.

They moved along the concrete paths, the children skipping on ahead, with Mildred beside Al as he pushed Dotty in the wheelchair. Bev and Dale settled behind them, enjoying a private moment. They wandered through the Gillette Visitors' Center and the butterfly garden, enjoying the colorful insects fluttering from flower to flower, occasionally even landing on the visitors.

Dale surprised Bev by pulling her away from the

others into a quiet lane. He guided her behind a broad tree trunk, then rested his hands on her shoulders and drew her close.

"Thanks so much for being part of this day. My mom loved the scarf, and I'm so happy you're here."

Bev wondered what had gotten into him. She studied his face, addled by the look in his eyes. "You don't have to thank me, Dale. I wouldn't have missed this for the world."

"You're amazing," he said, raising his hand to brush strands of hair from her cheek.

She felt the coolness of his fingers against her warm skin. Bewildered, she lowered her gaze, shy at his touch and the look in his eyes. The sunlight filtered through the leaves making dappled patterns on the ground. The fluttering of light and shadow patterned the same trembling in her chest.

When she lifted her head, Dale's gaze captured hers. "You add sunshine to my gloomy life, Bev."

Bev saw it happening. His mouth moved toward hers almost in slow motion. She held her breath, amazed at the sensations that charged through her. As his lips touched hers, the warmth and tenderness rolled across her like a gentle breeze.

When he drew back, a look of longing glinted in his eyes, and she felt the same within her heart. If only her life weren't so complicated. If only his weren't so filled with confusion. If only…

"We'd better get back," he said, taking her hand and drawing her into the sunlight.

Moments passed before Bev caught her breath, before she realized he'd really kissed her. She wished it could have lasted forever.

Ahead, she saw Al pushing Dotty's wheelchair, and she noticed the children craning their necks, probably looking for her. She hurried along so they wouldn't worry, and as she neared, Bev caught sight of Michael reaching toward a butterfly with its colorful outstretched wings.

"Don't touch it, please," she said to Michael. "If you brush the powder from its wings you can harm it."

Michael leaned closer and studied the insect. "What powder?"

"The color on their wings is their scales, and it's like powder. It helps them fly. So you have to be very careful."

He eyed her as if he didn't believe what she'd said, and she suspected as soon as she turned her back he'd brush one of the wings to check it out.

"Your mom's right," Dale said. "Butterflies can be injured when you touch their wings."

Michael's expression altered, and he listened as if Dale were the authority. The situation irked her, but she kept her mouth closed. Michael's behavior had improved, and she didn't want to jeopardize the changes.

"Do you like the butterflies?" Al asked, approaching Michael from a distance behind them.

Michael nodded. "You can't touch their wings or they can't fly."

"Good for you," Al said. "Most young fellows don't understand that."

"Dale told me," Michael said, grinning while Bev stewed.

As Bev watched Michael, he slipped his hand into Dale's, and Dale held it without maneuvering away. Her heart gave a lurch, validating what she already knew. As much as Dale meant to her, she'd allowed their relationship to go on too long. Her children were so open to being hurt.

"Dotty's getting tired," Al said, grasping the handles of her wheelchair and turning it to face the exit. Mildred joined them and moved on ahead with Kristin clinging to her grandmother's hand.

When Bev's attention returned to her son, Michael faltered a moment. "Will we ever have a dad?" His gaze drifted from Dale back to Bev.

Bev's heart stood still, and she felt her breath leave her. She took a moment to draw in some air. "You have a dad, Michael."

"He died, Mom."

"But he's still your father." She turned her gaze away from his pleading eyes.

"I mean will you ever get married so we can have a new one?"

"I don't know," Bev said, mortified by her son's question. "I doubt it."

Michael's expression faded to disappointment, but in a heartbeat, he rebounded. "But you don't know for sure."

She gave him a steady gaze, willing him to quiet.

"You never know life, Mom," Michael said, as if determined to get the last word in on the subject.

You never know life. His words poured over her like a cold shower. Life was always full of surprises for which she had no control. She picked up her pace, wanting to run away from her son's questions and Dale's probing look.

Dale stood in the doorway of his mother's bedroom watching her uneasy sleep. The day had been almost too much for her. She tired so easily that he was keenly aware this activity could be one of her last.

Dotty shifted and opened her eyes. "Where is everyone?"

"Dad went to the pharmacy for a few minutes to check on some things and the others went home."

"I'm sorry," Dotty said. "I get so tired now."

"I know."

"But I had a wonderful day, Dale. Thank you."

"You're welcome, Mom."

She patted the mattress beside her. "Sit with me. I'd like to talk."

He ambled forward. "Shouldn't you rest?"

"I had a catnap. I'll sleep again soon, but once in a while, I feel the need to talk about…things."

Dale's stomach knotted. What kinds of things? He slid onto the edge of the bed and took his mother's hand in his.

"Millie's a wonderful woman, Dale. When I see your dad and her together, I can't fathom why they weren't a couple in their younger years."

"It wasn't meant to be, Mom. They were friends."

"But can't you see the way your father's eyes light up when Millie's here? She's good for all of us. She makes us cheerful and keeps us from thinking about… about the future."

"Mom, please—"

"Dale, it's difficult, but we need to talk about these things. I don't want to head off to heaven without saying some things that are in my heart."

Dale cringed, hearing his mother's request. He didn't want to talk about the future. The present was difficult enough. He studied his mother's face and saw the need reflected in her eyes. "Go ahead, Mom."

She squeezed his hand. "Dale, I want your father to find a good Christian woman to make his life complete again."

He opened his mouth to protest, but his mother's look forced him to halt the words that rolled to his lips.

"Millie would be a perfect wife for your father. I've given it a lot of thought."

Nausea churned in Dale's stomach. He didn't want

to listen to his mother plan a romance for his father. The whole topic roiled inside him.

"Don't balk at this, please. I mean it. They share so much. They share a past, and now they share the present that's given us comfort. I know that the Lord has plans for your father's future. I can see it."

"Mom, you can't plan Dad's future. I know you like to take care of us, but this isn't the way to do it. Let's just focus on the present and—"

"And you, Dale. I'll never have grandchildren now, but I'd like to think that someday little souls will be born that are part of you. And if they're part of you, then they're part of me."

Her words ripped at his heart, and he had nothing to say, nothing to stop her from speaking her mind.

"Bev is a wonderful woman. I believe she'd make a loving partner and a good mother, and she has those two darling children."

Her look stopped him again.

"I've seen the good influence you've had on the boy. He needs a father, and he dotes on you, Dale. You're a hero in his eyes."

Hero. Dale felt about as far from a hero as he could get. He was a coward, really. He feared his mother's death. He feared commitment for the same reason. He had nothing to offer a woman like Bev. Though she'd seemed to enjoy his kiss earlier, he knew she had no long-term interest in him. She'd made that very clear.

Michael adored him, and Dale deserved none of it. All he could do was hurt the boy even more than life already had.

So what should he do now?

Dale fiddled with the piles of paper on his desk, his mind everywhere but on his job. He'd been weighted by his mother's words since her birthday. He didn't want to hear what she had to say, and he resented the thought of another woman walking into his father's life. Mildred had no business bursting into their lives and creating tensions at a time that was sensitive for them. Dale found the idea of a romance between Mildred and his father disquieting and couldn't believe his mother was contriving a relationship while she lay on her deathbed.

He'd also been rattled by Michael's conversation the same day. When the boy had asked Bev whether he'd ever have a father, Dale had panicked. The child had looked at him as if he were the answer. Dale had hoped never to be put in that position. He should have known that a kid wouldn't understand a friendship without thinking it had greater commitment. Sometimes he didn't understand it either.

Wisdom told him to get out of the situation even though he and Bev got along well. He enjoyed her company, and for the first time in many years he felt relaxed and content with a woman. Bev was easy to enjoy, but he wanted no part of a lifelong commitment.

Sometimes he played mind games by asking himself "what-if?," but as quickly as the question settled into his thoughts, he removed it. No what-ifs for him. He wanted no part of the heartache of a love relationship.

With Mildred still hanging around and caring for his mother, Dale felt tossed into the situation. How could he avoid Bev and her children when they were drawn into the family setting by his mother's or father's invitation?

The best he could do was stay away from them, and he'd tried. For the past three weeks, he'd avoided going home for the weekend. Instead, he'd dropped by for a couple of hours on Saturday or Sunday. He'd even missed visiting for the Fourth of July. No one needed him anyway. Mildred had taken over. She'd filled all of their needs, and Dale felt useless. Yet how could he continue to avoid going home with his mother so ill?

The telephone jarred him, and he snatched up the receiver, startled when he heard his father's voice.

"What's wrong?" Dale asked, his heart in this throat.

"I called to ask the same question. You've been coming home so faithfully on weekends, but you didn't show up this past week, not even for a few hours. I just wondered if you're okay."

The call coming so quickly on the heels of his thoughts set him on edge. "I'm fine, Dad. Sorry. I should have called." He tapped the pencil's eraser against his blotter as he scurried for something plausible to say.

"I'm tangled in a special project here, and I'm afraid it might be another week or so before I can get home."

"I'm disappointed to hear that," his father said. "Your mother misses you, but I understand. Your life goes on."

While his father's life halted. He finished the implication of his dad's words. Guilt slid over him like thick oil, turning his mood black.

"I'll see what I can do in another week or so. I should have things caught up by then." He hated the lie; it was not so much a lie as a half truth. He was busy, but that was nothing new. He could find the time when he needed it. If his mother died while he was playing hard to get, he'd never forgive himself. Dale flinched at the possibility.

"Don't push yourself, Son," his father said. "I know it's difficult to work and handle the pressures at home. Your mom asked about you, and I thought I'd better call."

"I'll telephone her tonight when I have a moment, Dad, so she's reassured."

"Thanks. She'll feel better."

Dale listened to his father's words, feeling shame and sadness. His father needed support, not a son who couldn't handle his own problems and took a coward's way out.

When Dale hung up the telephone, tears pushed behind his eyes, and he lowered his head in his hands. What can I do? he asked himself. Words filled his head. *Stand firm in the faith; be men of courage; be strong.*

Do everything in love. He recognized the Scripture. Bev. Since her prodding, he'd been reading the Bible and had touched on those verses a couple nights ago. In God's subtle way, the message he needed had been at the tip of his memory.

Be men of courage. He'd been so lacking in that. He'd lived in fear since he'd watched his mother go downhill, and he'd struggled with relationships since then. What had happened to his faith?

Do everything in love. He'd done little in the name of love. God's timing was what he had to deal with. We would all die one day. That was something he could not control.

He raised his head and pulled back his shoulders. *Lord, give me courage to be the hero Michael sees and help me to understand the kind of love You command.*

Love. He couldn't say the word aloud.

Chapter Eleven

Al closed the bedroom door and wiped his misting eyes with the backs of his hands. He'd promised the Lord thirty-seven years ago that he would love his wife in sickness and in health. He'd only been twenty-three then, but he'd meant it then as sure as he meant it today. No one had ever touched his heart as Dotty had done, and the only other person who'd come close was Millie.

Watching Dotty fail was almost more than Al could bear. Millie had stepped in to give him help and strength, and the Lord filled him with comfort, knowing Dotty's end would be a victory and not a loss.

But it would be his loss.

He wandered toward the living room, his mind filled with too many thoughts to handle. He leaned against the doorjamb and watched Millie gather the cups and plates from their dessert earlier in the evening.

"I'm worried," he said.

Mildred turned to face him, the china piled in her hand. "About Dotty?"

He nodded. "Dotty. Dale. Everything. Dale's not been coming home, but he called last night and said he'd be here this weekend."

"Dale's a good son," Mildred said. "He doesn't mean to hurt you. He's having a difficult time, too."

"I know, and I understand." He pushed his fingers against his eyes to hold back the welling tears. "Tonight Dotty said Dale couldn't face reality. Dotty knows…" He stopped, unable to say the words.

Mildred set the stack of dishes on the table and sank onto the sofa. She patted the cushion beside her. "Sit for a minute."

Al lumbered across the room, weighted by the pain of watching his world fall apart. When he sank beside Millie, she shifted to face him, and he saw the truth in her eyes.

"It's getting close," she said. "You need to be prepared."

Her words made his awareness a greater reality, and his chest heaved with an ache so deep it tore at his soul. "I know," was all he could say. He looked at Millie with blurred vision, then brushed the tears from his eyes.

"I wish I could give you more hope, but I have to be honest."

"I want you to be honest, no matter how it hurts."

She reached across and pressed her palm against his

hand. "I love Dotty. I ache for your grief, but I rejoice for her. Soon she'll be healthy and happy. No worries, no problems, no tears—only eternal joy. We should be envious."

A faint smile touched Al's lips, and the emotion shocked him. He hadn't smiled in days, even with Millie around to bring him a reprieve with her light-hearted ways. "Thank you," he said, knowing the words couldn't dent the gratefulness he felt.

She waved his thanks away.

"Millie, you've been a part of my life for so long. All the important things, and now—"

"That's what friends are for, Al. It's hard not to be sad even though we know Dotty will be with Jesus. It's difficult to accept the truth that God's will be done. I'm grateful I can be here during these last…these special days."

Special days. Only Millie would think of Dotty's last hours as special, and they were. The words rolled over him like a balm. "You're special, Millie. What would I do without you?"

"You have the Lord. That's all you need."

He nodded, his pulse throbbing with the painful knowledge of what he still had to bear.

Millie brushed her fingers against his cheek. "Your eyes look so sad. It hurts me to see you this way."

He pressed his palm against her warm fingers. "Then make me smile, Millie."

* * *

Bev pulled the bedsheets from the dryer and dropped them into the laundry basket to fold upstairs. While she untangled the linens from each other, her mind plodded through her weighty thoughts. She'd been on edge for the past two weeks, and didn't know what to do about it, or even why she'd let her life get as tangled with Dale's as badly as the sheets she'd been trying to unknot.

When Dale had called to say he was too busy to come for the weekend, she'd accepted what he'd said, but then it had happened again. She learned from her mother that he'd dropped by his parents' home for a couple of hours, but he hadn't visited her. He hadn't even called. Something was wrong and she'd wracked her memory, trying to figure out what she'd done or what had happened.

Dale's absence made Bev too aware of what part he now played in her life. He filled her days and nights with purpose and pleasure. She reveled in his kisses. For the first time in many years, she'd had a chance to think of herself and not just the children, and although she and Dale had declared their relationship a friendship, she'd watched it grow deeper and had begun to wonder if she could let go of her promise to herself never to marry. Lately, her heart had opened to a new desire to belong, to be a family, to share her life with someone.

The children were still a problem when it came to Dale, but even then, she'd noticed he had become more patient with them. She pictured him on the pier in Grand Haven with Michael in his arms, Dale's face twisted with the realization that her son had nearly fallen into the rough water.

She'd had reservations, too. If Dale were going to walk away—as he'd done now—then, for the good of the children, she needed to forget the delight she felt with him. She needed to slip back into her go-nowhere life and accept it again.

Bev slammed the dryer door closed and headed up the stairs with the clothes basket. Sorting through her muddied thoughts, she realized she'd gotten herself into the position she'd promised never to be in again. Dale had thrown her life off balance. Her stability had become rocky since she'd allowed her heart to head off in crazy directions. She needed to bind her emotions to reason.

The doorbell rang, and Bev set down the laundry. Before she could reach the door, another chime pealed from the foyer. Curious, Bev paused before turning the knob and glanced out the small, square window to see who was there. Her heart skipped.

"Dale," she said, pushing open the screen door. "Is something wrong?"

He shook his head, but his face looked grim.

She moved away from the door and waved him ahead of her into the living room. "Have a seat."

He didn't respond, but said as he sank onto the sofa, "I'm a mess, Bev." His face was filled with concern.

Bev sat across from him, confused by his sudden appearance. "What's going on?"

"I don't know, but I've certainly been a jerk. I should have let you know what's going on, and—"

"You're talking in circles, Dale. What's going on? I haven't seen you for three weeks or longer. Now you appear on my doorstep, and I'm confused."

"So am I, and that's why I haven't called or been around. I don't know what to say."

"Then why are you here?" She heard the sarcasm in her voice.

He glanced away, his face morphing from one emotion to another. "I don't know for sure. I want to let you know I care about you, but—" He drew his fingers through his thick hair.

His hesitation tore through her. "But what?"

"I care about you, but I don't want to."

His words struck her like a hypodermic needle—the puncture followed by a sting that lingered long after the needle had been withdrawn.

"That sounded so crass," he said. "So unkind."

"Yes, it does."

He leaned forward and rested his elbows on his knees, then folded his hands and stared at them. "You know all the reasons. I've told you how I feel about getting involved. I know life can't be perfect. That's heaven."

"You can't escape relationships unless you're a hermit, Dale. People need people. People form friendships. It's a natural thing. God made us that way."

"I have friends," he said. "I just don't want to fall in love."

"I don't either," Bev said, not sure she was telling the truth any longer. She only wished her dreams hadn't included Dale, but they clung to her like tape to paper.

He lifted his eyes and studied her face as if he were trying to read whether she was telling the truth. She stared back, garnering the strength to hide the deeper feelings she'd begun to experience.

He released a lengthy breath. "But the kids. I'm afraid they don't understand. I don't want to hurt them."

"I know you don't. The problem is children have vivid imaginations."

He nodded and fell back against the cushion. "Michael wants a father."

So that was it. She knew Dale had heard him at the Star-Spangled Butterfly Festival, but at the time, he hadn't reacted. "I've explained that to him. Michael has God the Father. The Lord is the only father he needs."

"Where are the kids?" he asked.

"Michael needed folders for school. My mom took him out to buy them."

She noticed him glance toward the hallway. "Kristin went with them."

He nodded, seemingly not surprised that she'd known his concern.

"We're alone."

"It's not only the kids, Bev. I'm going through some very immature feelings that I need to get under control."

"What kind of feelings?"

He lowered his eyes, his face drawn. "It's so childish, but I understand where the feelings are coming from."

"Explain, please." His avoidance irritated her.

"It's your mother. She's taken over and I feel so helpless. I'd like to do something for my folks, but I don't have a chance. Millie's already done everything. She's already thought of it before I do."

"You wanted someone to be a caregiver, someone to help your dad. Didn't you think that's what she'd do?"

Dale gave a faint shrug. "I figured she'd help feed Mom and stay with her, but your mother's almost moved in. She's there all the time. We have no time together. Alone."

Bev gave a ragged sigh. She'd seen the problem coming and her mother hadn't liked it when she'd pointed it out. "I can't control my mother. I did warn her."

Dale's head flew upward. "You did?"

"I saw the tension, and you'd hinted how you felt before. She won't listen. As long as she's nursing Dotty, my mom is very defensive. She sees it as her job."

"I know, and my father doesn't see the problem, so I don't know why it's bothering me. Like I said, it's childish. I'm the little boy vying for my parents' attention, but it's more than that. They've done so much for me that I want to give something back to them, and she's not letting me do that."

"Your love and your presence is all they need, Dale."

He looked away and didn't speak for a moment. "You're probably right," he said finally. "My dad will need me after my mom…"

He apparently couldn't say the words and neither could Bev. It was too sad, too disheartening. The whole situation sat on her shoulders like a boulder. All she wanted now was honesty.

"So where do we go from here?"

He gave her a long thoughtful look. "I miss you too much when we're apart, Bev. I don't want our friendship to end because I can't handle things. So let's start over again."

Start over again? They'd hardly started at all in her mind. "Start what over?"

"Us. Our friendship. Let's back up and get our emotions in check."

Bev closed her eyes a moment, realizing she'd been trying to do that all along, so what good would backing up do? "How do we back up?"

"We need to untangle ourselves from our families if that's possible. Let's keep the issues separate."

Bev still didn't understand, unless he was saying he didn't want anything to do with her kids and Mildred. She was in the dark.

"I'm thinking we should do some things alone as

friends do. Go to dinner or a movie alone. Get uninvolved from each other's families."

She'd been right. That's exactly what he'd meant. "It's not realistic, Dale. Maybe it's best if we just end things here and now. Friends are only worth the effort when it's give and take, when they enjoy each other's company. When the relationship is more stressful than pleasant, then give it up." She said the words, but her heart felt as if it were breaking.

Dale rose from his chair and moved to Bev's side. He captured her hands in his, then pressed them to his chest. "That's not what I mean, Bev. All I'm trying to say is we need to be friends again, and we need to try to get rid of all the confusion. I need you, and I hope you need me. I want to learn more about you outside the realm of our confusing lives. We haven't given us a chance."

Bev looked into his eyes, struck by his words. That seemed the most intelligent thing Dale had said since he'd arrived. Maybe they hadn't given themselves a chance at a real friendship.

"What do you say?" he asked.

She nodded. "I think you're right. We need time to explore our relationship without the pressures."

He lifted her hands to his lips and kissed her fingers. His lips felt warm and tender, and tonight, she let the emotion transport her to a sense of wholeness. Everyone needed a solid friendship. She and Dale had been on a slippery climb since they'd met.

"I haven't felt this good in weeks," Dale said, sliding his arm around her shoulders. "Things will be different from now on."

Bev's heart lurched, praying the difference would be a good one. She felt positive about their talk, but something troubled her, and she wasn't sure what it was. Could the Lord be trying to speak, and she wasn't hearing? Was it a woman's intuition?

Her mind had woven through a labyrinth of questions. Why did she dream now of being loved again? Why did she allow herself to hope for more when she'd resolved that a single life was the best? Would life be any different if she opened her heart? And if she did, what good would it do? Dale wanted friendship. If that's all they shared, would that be enough?

May the God of hope fill you with all joy and peace as you trust in him. The verse settled on her mind. Maybe it all boiled down to trust. Could she trust herself?

Could she trust Dale?

Al had pulled the chair beside Dotty's bed. Each time he rose to go, he feared that if he walked away she would leave him. He'd faced reality and tried to be prepared, but nothing would ready him for the moment when Dotty was no longer part of his life.

Her eyelids fluttered, and a soft moan stole from her throat.

"Do you need a pill?" Al asked, leaning closer to her ear.

She inched open her misted eyes. "No." Her voice was hoarse and strained.

He bent and kissed her fingers as they rested on the blanket.

Earlier, when it had still been light, Al had watched the burnished September leaves drift from the changing trees and flutter to the earth—part of life—an ending, yet a beginning. Dried foliage fed the earth, and in spring, flowers, grass and trees were reborn. He figured the cycle was somewhat like dying.

Al listened to Dotty's struggling breathing, his heart in his throat. As his eyes moistened, he sent a prayer heavenward. *Father, you can do all things. You can heal and you can end life. Help me to accept Your will. Help me to see hope for the future. I know Dotty's life is not ending, but beginning—like the leaves. Be with Dale and me, and I thank you for Millie who's brought sunshine into our gloomy lives during this difficult time. In Jesus's name.*

As his amen wafted into the air, Dotty's voice broke the silence. "I'm tired, Al. I want the Lord to take me home. Would you pray for that?"

Al hung his head and fought the desire to say no. "Dotty. Please…" The words caught in his throat.

"No, listen. I love you. We've had a grand life together. I—"

"Save your strength. I know you love me. I love you more than I can say."

"Be happy, Al. When I'm gone, your life will go on. I want you to be happy."

Be happy. The words shot through his heart like an arrow. "How can I be—"

"I want you to find love again—a woman like Millie."

"Don't say that. How can you even think of something like that?"

"You're such good friends, and I understand. I love her, too." She paused a moment as if catching her breath. "I don't know why God didn't…bring you two together years ago."

Al grasped her hand and pressed it to his cheek. "Because I wouldn't have loved you, Dotty."

"Millie will keep you strong, Al, when the time comes."

Her hand felt cold against his face, and she released a deep sigh that charged through Al's senses. He kissed her fingers, then lowered her hand to the blanket.

How much longer?

Only God knew the answer.

No matter. He would watch and wait. He would love her every minute of every day. Al knew of nothing else he could do.

"Ashes to ashes and dust to dust."

The pastor's voice carried on the breeze as he sprinkled Dotty's casket with earth.

"The Lord bless her and keep her. The Lord make His face shine on her and be gracious to her. The Lord look upon her with favor and give her peace." He closed the book as the mourners uttered an amen.

Dale scanned the blurred faces of those who gathered, then wiped the tears from his eyes. Neighbors, church family, relatives he hadn't seen in years had all come to pay tribute to his mother. While Dale sat on his father's left, Mildred sat on his right.

Bev and the children stood across from them. Bev's eyes were downcast while the children stared wide-eyed at the closed bronze casket. Inside, his mother rested on a cream-colored satin lining that gave her pale skin a warm glow. Dale knew she was happy and content, finally standing face to face with God, but for him and his father, the joy couldn't puncture the sense of loss.

The funeral home had been filled with flowers—bouquets in autumn hues, planters and baskets brimming with life while his mother lay cold in their midst. Her life had ended without fanfare. She'd died in her sleep while his father sat by her side.

Tears dripped to Dale's fingers. He pulled out his handkerchief and brushed them away with an angry swipe.

No bitterness, he told himself. God's will be done, but his heart still struggled with the Lord's will. Dale would survive. He'd be back in Grand Rapids, but what about his father? Certainly, he would return to work. The pharmacy would keep him busy. He'd probably throw himself into church activities. Anything and everything to fill the empty space and deep silence that would be his life.

He tuned in to the pastor's voice—the Lord's Prayer and the benediction. The funeral director stepped forward, inviting everyone to the church for a luncheon. Luncheon? How could he eat?

The mourners filed past the casket, some taking a flower from the spray, others patting the cold metal coffin. Ian and Esther moved past. Annie and Ken. Bev had mentioned Annie was expecting, and Dale let his gaze drift to her belly. Death and birth. Part of the cycle.

The Hartmann sisters who owned the Loving Arms boardinghouse shuffled past—Abby and Sissy, their white hair looking almost blue in the morning light.

Bev stepped forward, and he watched as she pressed her hand against the cold bronze metal while the children clutched their hands together as if they feared touching anything would place some horrible spell over them.

Finally only his father and he remained. And Mildred. He longed to ask her to leave, to let his father and him spend the last moments alone, but he stopped himself. Mildred wasn't at fault. Life was. Once a person was born, he had to die. That was part of the deal.

Before he anguished over the situation any longer, Mildred gave his father a pat and moved from beneath the graveside canopy.

He joined his father beside the casket, not knowing what to say or what to do.

His father rested both hands against the icy metal and drew in a ragged sigh. "I'll love you always, Dotty."

Dale placed his hand on his father's shoulder. "She loved you so much, Dad."

"And you, too, Son."

"We'll manage somehow."

He nodded. "Your mom said Millie would get me through this."

Dale felt his back stiffen. "God will get you through it, Dad."

His father gave a single nod, then turned away and stepped from beneath the canopy into the sunlight.

Dale watched as his father strode toward Mildred. Bev stood back, her face taut with sadness. He saw Michael searching his face, and to alleviate the boy's fears, Dale strode across the grass and gave the child a hug. Kristin moved closer, and he included her in the embrace.

"We'd better go," Bev said, giving the kids a pat.

Dale straightened and gestured toward the black limousine waiting for him. "I'll see you back at church."

She nodded.

He took a step toward his father, then realized he'd invited Mildred to ride in the car with them. Dale bit back his resentment. He forced his legs to carry him forward. He'd handle the problem another day. Today wasn't the time.

Chapter Twelve

Bev noticed a difference in Dale after his mother died. He still came home to spend time with his father, but she'd heard him grumble often that his dad didn't need him. Bev realized that her mother and Al were spending a great deal of time together since Dotty had died. Too much time, although it seemed innocent enough. But Bev wondered if others saw it the same way she did.

Dale didn't. He resented it.

She eyed her watch, expecting Dale to arrive any minute. The kids were visiting with school friends down the block, and Bev was enjoying one of the quiet moments she rarely experienced.

Kristin had begun kindergarten a few days after Dotty's funeral, and though it was difficult to see her baby grow up, Bev felt pleased that Kristin loved school and had made so many new friends in the past month.

A sound came from the front door, and Bev headed for it, expecting Dale. Instead her mother burst in, her cheeks rosy from the October breeze and her eyes glowing as if something special had happened.

"I found it," she said, dropping her handbag on the sofa. She plopped down beside it with a wry look.

"You found what?"

"An apartment. Al and I stumbled on it by accident."

Bev's concern about her mother's attachment to Al rose, but even more, she pondered how packing up Dotty's clothes could have resulted in locating an apartment.

After a rambling story of how she'd learned about the apartment, her mother finally got to the meat of the topic. "It's a first-floor apartment on Packwood Drive. It's perfect. Al wrote the deposit check, and I'll pay him back."

An edgy feeling coursed through Bev. "I'm glad, Mom, but that was a quick decision. Maybe you should have let me look at it before you settled on that one."

"Why? We liked it." She rose and picked up her handbag. "You and Dale need space. You have no privacy when I'm here."

"I don't need privacy with Dale."

"I know. You're just friends." Mildred gave a harrumph. "But like Al said one day, the best marriages are made up of good friends first."

The comment irked Bev.

"Mom, don't you think you're spending too much

time with Al?" Bev asked, thinking more of Dale than of her own concerns.

"Why?"

"People will talk."

"What people? I haven't heard a word." She slid her arm through the handle of her purse. "We're friends, Bev. You don't walk out on a friend when he needs you."

"I know, Mom." She sorted her thoughts, wishing she could explain. "But people talk."

"Then it's their problem, not mine," Mildred said. "Al's lonely, Bev. He's hurting. We both miss Dotty and spending time together helps us. Do you expect me to neglect a friend because someone might gossip?"

"No, but I—"

"I see nothing wrong with it."

Bev opened her mouth to respond, but the doorbell stopped her, followed by Dale's call from the doorway.

"Come in," Bev said.

He pushed open the door and strode in, halting when he spied her mother. Fearing he'd make a comment, Bev sent him a quick frown.

He gave a subtle tilt of his head as if he understood. "What's up?"

"Mom's rented an apartment."

"Congratulations," he said to Mildred.

"Thanks. I hope you can help me on moving day."

"Sure." He turned to Bev. "Do you like it?"

"I haven't seen it. She was with your dad."

Dale's expression altered.

Mildred took a step toward the hallway. "I suppose I should start making a list of everything I have to do. I have most of my things in storage. I'll have to contact the storage company." She rattled on about what she needed to do and what she needed to buy until she finally went to her room.

Dale sank onto the sofa and looked at Bev. "Come sit with me." He patted the cushion beside him. "Let's forget all that." He waved toward her mother's room.

She ambled to his side and sank into the cushion, frustrated and certain he was, too.

Dale took her hand in his. "I wanted to spend time with you, but it's not happening." He gave her a helpless look. "We need to make some changes, Bev. I've been adamant about just being friends, but maybe I was wrong."

Her heart kicked against her ribs. "Why the change?"

His head drooped as if trying to formulate his thoughts.

Bev lifted her free hand and turned his downcast face toward hers. "This is important, and I need to understand."

He covered her hand with his. "I'm realizing a friendship can deepen. It doesn't stay stagnant. It grows into something special. Look at my dad. He's grieving, but I see him smile when Millie shows up…which is much of the time."

Bev held up her hand. "Let's not get into that, please."

"I'm trying to accept it, Bev, but it's us I'm talking about." His thoughtful gaze drifted over her. "You make me happy, too. But have you realized that we're never alone? Since Mom died, we're always with someone."

"That's true," she said, thinking of their parents and her kids.

"Tomorrow's the Autumnfest in town. How about going? Just you and me?"

She found her voice. "Just the two of us?"

Though he smiled, she noticed the sincerity in his eyes.

"All right. I'd like that." Her voice sounded soft and breathy.

He tightened the pressure on her hand. "I'm changing, Bev. I see things differently now. I hope you feel the same."

"I don't know how I feel anymore," she said.

Dale's face darkened, and she was sorry for saying what she had. But she felt on a whirlwind with Dale, never knowing which way he would head and what he could destroy in the process.

"I like you a lot, Dale. You're in my thoughts so often, but I'm nervous about this. I agree we haven't explored who we are when we're not under stress."

"Are you willing to take a chance on me?"

The question washed over her like the tide, pulling and pushing her thoughts, but always settling back where her heart lay. She nodded. "I'm willing to take a chance if you are."

He cupped her face in his hands as his eyes searched hers, then they lowered to her lips. Her pulse skipped through her. He closed the distance between them, his lips reaching hers.

"Mom!"

The door slammed and footsteps pounded through the kitchen.

Bev sighed as disappointment rolled through her. "We do have a long way to go."

Dale gave a crooked grin. "But it's worth it."

Bev prayed he was right.

"Let's sit and have a soda," Dale said, motioning to a food booth set up for the Grand Haven Autumnfest. The evening had felt strange, but wonderful. He and Bev had done many things together, but this time they'd been alone—no family, no friends, no kids—on a regular date. Since his mother's death, Bev had been Dale's rock. She'd listened to his sorrow and had seen him cry. Until recently, a date had seemed as far-fetched to him as mountain climbing and probably as dangerous. Tonight the thought made him grin.

Bev sank onto a bench near the boardwalk as he headed for the booth and returned with two cold drinks. He gave her one, then sat beside her.

Dale looked toward the water, admiring the sun as it spread its gold across the lake. He and Bev sipped their soft drinks, saying little, and watched the fiery orb rest upon the water, then slide below the horizon in a splash of brilliant colors.

In the quiet, Dale's thoughts gripped him. Sometimes he'd felt as if Bev had wheedled her way into his life and made it difficult for him to escape. But he knew better. He'd opened himself for the attraction. He'd let his empty life become filled with the confused world of a woman and her children. Now he felt incomplete without them.

"Haven't you ever wanted to be married again, Bev?"

Hearing his question startled Dale, and he wished he hadn't asked it. "I know you said you'd never do it again, but haven't you even considered what it might be like?"

Bev became thoughtful before she faced him. "I didn't for years, but now that Kristin's in school, I've had thoughts."

He slipped his arm around her back and breathed in her sweet fragrance. He wanted to hear more but was afraid to push.

She was quiet for a moment, her face serious in the fading light. "I don't know why. The kids are growing up so fast. Sometimes I ask myself what it would be like to have another child. I love babies, and in a few years, I'll be too old to be a mother. Mothering takes energy."

Another child. The idea spun in his mind.

"Then I think about spending years alone. I always figure God meant people to be in twos. Like the ark." She shifted to face him. "What about you?"

"You mean about my having children?"

"Children. Marriage. You've always said you'd never marry."

"The thought's crossed my mind." His heart picked up pace at his admission. "Marriage has pros and cons. It seems to intensify everything."

"Good things always have a negative. A good dinner means too many calories or maybe heartburn. That's the way life is. I've avoided relationships, too, afraid that things wouldn't work."

She lifted her drink and took a sip. "When I married Jesse, I made the promise for better or worse, but in my heart, I expected better. Worse seemed impossible, but I guess I didn't know Jesse well enough. He loved his motorcycle. He loved going out and taking chances without thinking about us. I lived in fear. Then one day, my fear came to fruition. I often felt guilty, wondering if my lack of faith had caused the accident."

Dale reeled with her comment. "Things don't work that way, Bev. You know better than that. How many times have you told me the Lord doesn't give us problems? He gives us choices."

Courage charged through Dale as the feelings he'd kept hidden seemed to surface. "I've struggled with my feelings for you, but I've lost the battle. My life seems empty when we're apart. I wonder what you're doing, and I pick up the telephone to call, then I put it down because it all seems so hopeless."

She frowned as if she didn't understand.

"But not anymore. I've changed, and I want to see where things will go with us," he said.

"We've both changed, but I'm afraid we have some insurmountable differences."

Her words felt like a kick in the gut. "Nothing is insurmountable."

"I have children. Two of them. That's a difference we can't ignore."

He lifted her hand in his and clutched it to his chest. "Things are happening inside me, Bev. I keep thinking about the day Michael almost slipped off the pier. I held him in my arms unable to deal with the thought that he could have been hurt."

"That was one day, Dale. The year has three hundred and sixty-five."

He grasped her shoulders and drew her closer. "Will you give me a chance, Bev? Will you give *us* a chance?"

"Words are one thing. Action is another. I need to see it, Dale."

"What must I do to make you believe me?"

"You know how I feel about my children. Let me see the change in your relationship to them." She drew back and grasped his arms. "I'll be honest with you. My feelings toward you have been growing for a long time, but I wouldn't let myself love you because I refuse to hurt my children again."

Dale's heart thudded as he listened. Her feelings

had been growing for a long time, and he hadn't believed it. He looked into her misted eyes and saw sincerity. Music floated to them on the evening air, and he rose.

"Trust me, Bev. I'll be a new man."

"Promise?"

"Promise." He reached out to take her hand. "Let's head back to the bandstand."

She gave him a tender smile, then placed her hand in his and stood. Dale slipped his arm around her shoulders as they wandered toward the music. Streetlights came on as they walked, brightening the dusky light of evening. As they neared the dancers, Dale urged her forward. He wrapped his arm around her waist and clasped her hand, allowing the soft lilting music to muffle the sounds of the passersby.

They glided to the rhythm of the love song as he breathed in the scent of lake breeze blended with Bev's fragrance. His cheek rested against her hair, and his heart tripped as he ran his hand over the small of her back.

A cool breeze blew in from across the lake, ruffling the fabric of her skirt and penetrating his cotton shirt. He nestled her closer, their bodies swaying as their feet moved.

When the song ended, Dale managed to let her go, desiring to hold her forever and wishing their lives could glide as smoothly as their dancing.

She gave him a timid smile. "Should we get going?"

"Probably," he said, reluctant to leave.

Heading back toward his car, Dale faced his concern. He was crazy about Bev. Why hide it anymore? But he'd promised to prove his love through her children. Could he be the kind of father they deserved? Dale knew he didn't dislike the kids. At times, he'd enjoyed them, but he was a novice, a selfish man who'd never learned to share. All he could do was pray that God give him the wisdom and patience he needed.

He guided Bev across the street, and as they walked a booth caught his eye. He looked above at the sign. Jenni's Loving Kisses. Chocolate candy lined the display cases. Pink boxes sat along the table. "What flavor are these?" he asked, pointing to the decorative designs that marked the top.

"They're truffles," the woman said. "These are almond. These are mocha. Here's mint."

"Truffles?"

"Creamy chocolate with flavoring on the inside and dipped in dark or milk chocolate."

"Would you like one?" Dale asked, turning to Bev.

"Do you have raspberry?" Bev asked.

The clerk nodded, pointing to a small bonbon marked by a white swirl across the top.

"I'll have one of those."

Dale selected one for himself, but his thoughts took a leap, and as he paid for the candy, he longed for a real kiss not a chocolate one, knowing nothing was sweeter than Bev's shapely mouth.

He took Bev's arm and wove his way through the crowd toward his car parked along a side street.

Once they were inside the sedan, Dale drew Bev closer. "How about another kiss?"

"No thanks, I've—"

He tilted her chin toward him. "Not Jenni's, the real thing."

Her smile sent his stomach reeling. Dale drew her into his arms as she tilted her face toward his. His mouth met hers, teased by the taste of raspberry chocolate lingering on her lips. But the sweet sensation was more than candy. Tonight he took his time, reveling in the exquisite feel of her lips against his, the gentle sensation that soared in his heart.

Dale gave his feelings full sway. He raised his palm and cupped her cheek, then ran his fingers through her silky hair. When he drew back, Bev gazed at him questioningly. He had no answers. His only thought was: Who needed Jenni's kisses when Bev's offered so much more?

Chapter Thirteen

Leaves skittered across the concrete sidewalk and crunched beneath Bev's feet. Though a cool wind blew from the north, her fingers felt warm clasped within Dale's strong hand. Autumn seemed like an ending—a time when things were dying and winter's bitter cold was ready to pounce upon humanity.

But today the November chill didn't affect Bev's greater sense of a new beginning. She and Dale had given up the battle and had joined forces. They'd both pushed aside past fears and allowed their true feelings to emerge like early-spring buds beneath the winter's snow.

The feeling warmed her. She looked at his strong profile, admiring the smile crinkles beside his eyes that she'd witnessed far more often these past days. When she could see him face to face, his eyes still mesmerized her.

They walked in silence with only the sound of the leaves rustling beneath their feet and the echoes of her children ahead of them, racing toward the park swings.

Dale squeezed her hand, then turned to give her a smile.

"What?" she asked.

He chuckled. "Is it that rare to see me smile?"

"Not anymore."

"I was thinking that you're terrific."

Her chest tightened, and when he squeezed her hand, his touch seemed to roll up her arm. "Why am I terrific?"

"How can you ask? You've put up with me. You've raised two great kids."

Bev felt a frown settle on her face and stopped. "What?"

"I'm beginning to appreciate them now that I've stopped fighting it."

He had done that. He'd run to the store for Michael's forgotten school equipment, he'd helped Kristin make cookies for her class—even though they were slice and bake. He'd made some changes. The only thing that really concerned her now was his attitude toward her mother, and she could hardly fault him. Bev felt nearly the same.

"No reservations at all?" she asked.

His smile faded, and he stood beside her swishing the burnished leaves with the toe of his boot. The look concerned her, and she was almost sorry she asked.

"Do you want me to be truthful?" His full lips straightened to a narrow slit.

The tension tore through Bev like a gale, and she shifted away. His question gave her the answer. He had reservations. "Yes," was all she said.

He grasped her arms and turned her to face him. "I'm learning, Bev. I care about you more than words can say, and the kids are growing on me. I realize that along with the problems they can be pure fun."

Bev let his words wash over her. Dale and she had spent a great deal of time together in the past weeks. His affection had blossomed, and her longing for them to be a family had grown. Today she realized that her worst fear could happen again. "Thanks for your honesty."

"No, please, don't misunderstand. I'm following my heart. You're everything to me."

She knew it was coming so why not get it out in the open? "But?"

"But sometimes my head and heart aren't agreeing."

"And that's supposed to comfort me?" Her self-pity slipped away, replaced by frustration.

"Bev, please, I'm being honest. Give me time, and I promise you—"

"The only promises I can trust, Dale, are the Lord's. God won't abandon us. That's what's important."

Dale's heart gave a kick. If he walked out on them, it would be the same as Jesse betraying Bev and the children with his death. He could never do that. "I won't abandon you, Bev."

She looked at him with doubt in her eyes.

Remorse flooded Dale. Bev filled his heart and mind. Why had he admitted to her that he still struggled at times with commitment? What did he fear? And why?

Longing filled him. Whether his head knew it, his heart had no doubt. He wanted to spend his life with Bev. He'd learned so many things from her, things that helped him to be a better man.

Dale gave a quick glance behind him. The children were on the swings and no one appeared in the distance. "Bev, trust me, please."

Her sad gaze captured his, and, as if she were looking into his soul, she gave him a faint nod. "I'll trust you, Dale, but it's not just me. It's Michael and Kristin."

"I understand," he said. And for once, he truly did.

His lips met hers, washing him in summer heat. Though cold to the touch, they warmed against hers. A part of Scripture he'd read a few nights earlier flew into his thoughts. *If two lie down together, they will keep warm. But how can one keep warm alone?* Dale had been alone too long.

He drew Bev closer, his body tensing with his earlier admission. How could he ever say goodbye? Why would any man walk away from this amazing woman who'd awakened his emotions and dragged them from hiding?

Bev leaned into his kiss, her mouth moving against his, her hand raking through his hair. Her kiss filled his emptiness with sweet longing and took his breath away.

He drew back, knowing his face said it all, said the words so difficult for him to speak—I love you.

Michael's voice broke through their silence, and Dale pivoted to look across the leaf-strewn grass to the playground. The child's smile lit the day, and he beckoned to them.

"Dale, come and push us," the child called. The boy had forgotten Dale's unpleasant manner of the past. Now his face glowed with innocent trust and faith.

Dale gave Bev a hug, then cut across the grass. The faith of a child, Dale thought as he neared the children. That's how he needed to approach God. Maybe that was the same philosophy with marriage. A child didn't go through life worrying whether a problem might occur tomorrow. A child stepped into life full-tilt with the desire to grow and learn. Bev and her children couldn't be blamed for his constant fears and concerns.

"What's up?" Dale asked as he approached Michael.

"I want you to push me." He tilted his face toward Dale's, then sent him a hesitant smile. "Please."

Dale's heart ached, and he tousled the boy's hair. "That's why I'm here."

He gave the swing a hearty push, and Michael flew upward, his laughter greeting Dale's ears and making him smile. He didn't neglect Kristin. She'd always been a good girl, a sweet child who'd drawn him enough pictures to cover three refrigerators.

He gave her swing a thrust and heard her giggle as

he moved back to Michael with another gigantic shove that sent the boy higher than before. Dale glanced over his shoulder and saw Bev watching them from a park bench. Her face glowed in the autumn sun. She pulled her hand from a pocket and gave him a wave, then tucked it back inside. He beckoned her, but she shook her head and grinned.

"Ever tried the horizontal ladder?" Dale asked, as the swing slowed to a halt.

The boy eyed him suspiciously, then checked out the equipment. "No," he said finally.

"Me neither," Kristin said.

Dale realized why the boy had never used the horizontal ladder. He had no dad to lift him and give him direction. He beckoned to them, and they skipped beside him as if he were a balloon man.

"Okay. Who's first?" They hesitated, and Dale decided to make the choice. "Come on, Michael, let's see how strong you are."

He lifted the boy and helped him get a solid grip on the bars. Michael hung like deadweight with Dale's hands close at his sides until finally the boy swung his legs forward, then backward.

Dale stayed beside him, his hands supporting Michael's midsection. "Let go with one hand, and grab the next bar. I'll catch you if you fall."

He saw a questioning look in the child's eyes, but in a moment, Michael let go and grabbed the bar. The boy's sense of accomplishment eased through Dale's chest. "Good for you."

Michael beamed and tried another. After a failed attempt, Dale clutched his waist. "Had enough?"

Michael nodded, and Dale grasped the boy and set his feet on the ground. Dale wished he had the trust Michael had. Though leery, the boy took a chance and succeeded. Why couldn't Dale do the same?

"I did it," Michael said, checking to see if his mother had been watching.

She waved, giving him a thumbs-up.

"Mom saw me," Michael announced. "I did three."

"You did good," Dale said, resting his arm on the boy's thin shoulder. "Once you get some more muscles you'll do five or even six."

"Muscles like you?" Michael asked, eyeing Dale's jacket.

Dale lifted his arm in a he-man pose and listened to the children giggle. His focus drifted to Kristin, waiting with her arms reaching upward for her turn. "I think this might be too much for you, Kristin. Girls don't have nearly as much muscle as boys."

"Yes, they do," she said.

"No. They're just pretty." He winked at her and gave her ponytail a gentle yank.

"Girls aren't just pretty. Look," she said, making a muscle.

She gave him a playful frown. He realized his mistake and felt her slender arm. "That's pretty good muscle, but let's do something fun. How about the tube slide? I'll catch you at the bottom."

She didn't argue about that and ran toward the slide.

Dale followed and stood at the bottom of the huge red tube to catch Kristin and Michael as they shot from the plastic pipe. His heart lifted with their simple pleasure. Swings, slides and monkey bars. If life could only be that simple.

He stood back a moment breathing in the brisk air, filling his lungs with oxygen and his heart with hope. He'd made one step forward. Tomorrow he'd make another. He gave the kids a pat, then turned his eyes toward Bev. As he walked toward her, he sent up a prayer—a renewed gift he'd learned from Bev. Prayer might not be answered right away, but he knew God heard, and he trusted the Lord would answer him eventually.

"Where do you want this, Mom?"

Bev held a carton of knickknacks against her hip. She gazed around the apartment living room and could not conceive of what her mother planned to do with all her memorabilia. Mildred had done a good job of disposing of furniture, but she'd clung to her memories.

"Just put them in a corner," she said. "I'll figure out something."

Bev shifted the box to the other side and trudged across the floor. Though the carpet had seen better days it appeared to be clean, and a few strategically placed scatter rugs would cover up the worst of it.

She kept thinking of her talk with Dale at the park. His honesty had stung her at first, and then she forced herself to step back and accept what he said. Dale had made great strides. She had known from the beginning how he felt, just as she had reservations. The difference was, her fears had faded more quickly than his.

She didn't totally understand what bothered him, but as she thought about it, she found some sense in his fears. She'd been married once. She'd been twenty-two when she and Jesse had married. Young, naive, ready for adventure. Dale was thirty-six and had never married. He'd been an only child, never having to share his toys or his parents. They'd doted on him. He'd watched his parents' perfect love, which turned into the belief that he could never find a soul mate the way his parents had. Now he had to face a new truth, and it hurt.

The doorbell rang, jarring Bev's thoughts. She heard her mother's exclamation, too, and at the sound, Dale came from the bedroom, perspiration beading his forehead. "Setting up that bed ain't easy."

Mildred pulled open the door and backed away, a grin spreading over her face. "What are you doing here?"

Al strutted in with a wry smile. "The best medicine .

is keeping mind and body busy. I had someone fill in for me at the pharmacy."

"Really?" Dale drew back in surprise. "Mom had to beg you to get out of there on a Saturday."

"I'm older and wiser," Al said, giving his son a tilt of the head. He panned the room, then looked down the hallway. "Where are the kids?"

"They're at Annie's," Bev said, grateful that Annie was willing to keep an eye on them. Annie's pregnancy had drawn her and Bev closer together, a friendship they both needed.

"I suppose having them underfoot today wouldn't be a good idea." Al looked around the room at the piles of boxes, then tucked a hand into his pants pocket and jingled his change. "So what can I do to help?"

Dale gave a sweeping gesture toward the bedroom. "Be my guest. I can't set up that bed by myself. It weighs a ton."

"That's how good furniture was made," Mildred said. "Good, solid hardwood. None of that veneer-covered plywood they have nowadays."

The men vanished into the bedroom, and Mildred chuckled. "I knew he'd come."

Bev didn't like the girlish giggle. "You mean Al?"

She nodded. "He really needs to keep busy. He thinks too much at the pharmacy."

Bev opened her mouth, then disengaged her comment and opened another box. Inside, she spotted her mother's towels. Glad for an opportunity to get away from the conversation, Bev headed for the linen closet, but her mother followed.

"Al spent the last few years totally immersed in Dotty's illness," Mildred said, padding along behind her. "He used to read and golf. He watched sports. I don't think he does any of that now. He just thinks." She pulled towels from the carton and slid them onto a shelf.

"You were like that when Dad died," Bev said, folding a mussed tablecloth.

"No, not totally. Dad's illness was brief. It was awful, no question, but my life didn't revolve around his care for years before he died. Al needs to rebuild his life."

And you're planning to help him, Bev thought. She worked quietly beside her mother, letting her ramble about Al and Dotty. Her mother's life had gotten twisted with theirs, and Bev felt her mom had lost her independence. The relaxed retirement Mildred had planned had ended the day she began caring for Dotty.

The next hour slipped by with little talk from the men except their grunts and groans as they moved pieces of furniture. Bev's mother could never settle on an arrangement, and finally Al caved into a chair and protested.

"We need to plot this out, Millie, my girl. You're working with one young bull and one old rhino. I'm not able to hoist this stuff around."

"Sorry," Mildred said. "You know me. I don't always think ahead."

Al gave a chuckle as he lifted a sofa pillow and pitched it at her.

She looked startled, but caught it in midair. She laughed and tossed it back.

Al reached out, grasped her hand and tugged her down beside him. "See," he said, "this woman keeps my mind off my sadness. Nothing wrong with that."

Bev tried to smile, but the tension in her face felt like an overstretched balloon. Dale tucked his hands in his pockets and turned away. He walked to the window and looked outside.

Mildred jumped up and smoothed her blouse. "Let me fix some lunch. Anyone for a sandwich?"

Al raised his hand. Dale spun around. "Me, too," he said. A look of reprieve washed over his face.

"I'll help," Bev said and followed her into the kitchen.

Dale watched them go. He'd managed to contain himself as they worked, but his concern had risen sky-high as he watched the older couple's playful antics. His father pattered around like a young buck. His dad had been downcast for so long while his mother was ill, now Dale resented his father bouncing back from his loss. What had happened to the love and devotion he'd admired?

The two men sat a moment in silence until Al cleared his throat.

Dale peered at him, recognizing the familiar trait.

"Something on your mind?" Dale asked.

"I've been thinking."

"About what?"

"I'm thinking I should retire. Life is too short to waste on working. How much money does a man need?"

Dale clamped his mouth closed, afraid of what he'd say if he responded.

His father eyed him. "What do you think?"

"Don't ask me, Dad. You don't want to hear what I have to say."

"Say it." His father rose, walked to the center of the room and turned to face him. "Go ahead."

"Why didn't you retire when Mom was alive? She needed you then, and you worked every day."

Al drew in a breath that rattled through his chest. "It never entered my mind. Seemed I needed to work."

"But Mom was alone in the early days when she was first diagnosed, and later, you spent time running back and forth from the pharmacy to the house. It doesn't make sense to retire now."

His father looked at him with blank eyes. "Maybe it doesn't." He rubbed the back of his neck, moving it as if to relax the tension. "I guess it doesn't make sense to you."

"You're right. You need something to fill your time now. If you retire what will you do?"

"I'll enjoy myself, I suppose." He ambled across the room and sank back into the chair.

"What's gotten into you?" Dale stood above his father, studying his face. His chest ached from the stabbing emotions.

A look of surprise lifted Al's eyebrows. "What do you mean? I'm trying to live the few years I have left."

"You're acting like a kid. Mom just died a few weeks ago. Shouldn't you be in mourning?"

Al stood and glanced toward the kitchen, then faced Dale. "Don't you think I'm grieving, Dale?" His voice grew louder. Apparently realizing that, he lowered it. "Do you want me to walk around with tears rolling down my cheeks? I did plenty of that while I watched your mother suffer and fade from my life."

"I know," Dale said, backing away from his father's scowl. "I just mean that people don't see what's in your heart. They see how you're acting."

"Let's get this straight. Your mother will always have a piece of my heart. She'll never leave me, but she's not here anymore, Son. She's in heaven, and I'm here on earth. Your mom and I talked about this. She told me to be happy when she's gone. To get on with my life. I'm not doing anything more than your mom asked, and Millie helps me do that."

Dale turned away, unable to respond. His father didn't understand that *he* wanted to fill that space. It was his right to give his father support, but Mildred didn't give him a chance.

Dale was needled by the possibility of his father and Mildred becoming a couple. The vision raked over him, leaving him recoiling. His mother had been gone such a short time. What had happened to that perfect love? That soul mate idea he'd had?

If his relationship with Bev continued to grow, he didn't want his father to end up being his father-in-law. The situation overpowered all reason. Somehow he needed to explain this to his father, but until he could do it without feeling the frustration that overwhelmed him, he would say nothing.

Bev sat beneath the hair dryer at the Loving Hair Salon and flipped through the pages of a magazine. The article she'd been reading had come to an abrupt halt when Bev reached a torn-out page. A recipe, she decided. She disliked people who had the audacity to rip pages from magazines in doctors' offices and beauty shops.

She dropped the magazine into her lap and closed her eyes, thinking about Thanksgiving dinner the day before. It had seemed special to have a houseful. Dale had been tremendous with the kids. He'd played a board game with them, and Al had joined in when she and her mother had left for the kitchen to finish cooking the dinner.

Bev had sensed a strain between Dale and his father. The tension surprised her, and she wished Dale would tell her what had happened between them. She'd learned to let Dale struggle with his problems alone until he was ready. They both had things to learn.

She had been taught one important lesson. If she followed God's leading, she had nothing to fear. Bev had struggled with her feelings for Dale. She'd held back. She'd lived in the past, afraid of the future, but the Lord had opened her eyes to new possibilities, and she'd trusted in Him. Her life was in God's gracious hands.

Bev nestled deeper into the salon chair and leaned back her head as far as it could go without pushing the curlers against her scalp. Sitting under a dryer was never comfortable.

Voices hummed around her, hidden behind the thrumming of the blower. Bev had noticed two women from Fellowship Church arrive after she had. Now they were seated nearby, and their voices lifted above the other shop noises.

"You'd think she'd have better sense than to make it so obvious," the older woman said.

Bev didn't know the woman's name, but she'd seen her at various church functions. The other, Mrs. Taylor, shook her head. "They're old friends, I think," she said. "Mildred's a Christian woman. She wouldn't do anything she thought was sinful."

When Bev overheard her mother's name, her pulse kicked up a notch. She turned her head away so they wouldn't notice her, but kept an ear aimed toward them and gave full attention to their conversation.

"Old friends or not, I suspect some hanky-panky. His wife's been in the grave for little more than a month."

Bev winced, hearing the woman's suggestive comment.

"We don't know how we'd react if we lost our husbands, Marge," Mrs. Taylor said. "We really can't judge."

Marge, Bev thought, having wondered about the other woman's name.

Marge's voice rose in pitch so the tone penetrated the roar in Bev's ears. "Do you think I'm judging? I'm not. I'm only reporting what I see. I've seen them in restaurants together. They giggle like teenagers. I've even seen them shopping. Goodness, what do you expect a person to think?"

"They're friends. Wouldn't you help a friend in need?"

Marge rolled her eyes. "In need of what?"

Bev recoiled at the innuendo in the woman's voice.

"They sit together in church, of all things," Marge said. "I saw them again at the Thanksgiving service. Seems like they're tossing their sin in everyone's faces."

"Church is where all of us sinners belong," Mrs. Taylor said, stressing the word *us*. "Ye who are without sin cast the first stone."

She couldn't hear it, but Bev could tell Marge was huffing and puffing at Mrs. Taylor's comment.

Bev clamped her jaw, riled by what she'd heard. Mrs. Taylor had tried to skew the facts into something positive, but the woman named Marge would have no part of it. Gossip. Bev had seen it coming, but now what would she do about it? Her mother would have no part in listening to Bev's warnings.

Anger and frustration competed inside Bev. Anger at the woman. Frustration with her mother.

Dale disliked the situation, too. He hadn't said much, but Bev saw it in his behavior. Lately he seemed to avoid her mother. When they were together, Dale didn't talk much. He stood off and stared out the window. That seemed to be his way of coping.

Mrs. Taylor's comments about sitting in judgment pressed against Bev's thoughts, and she realized she and Dale were also guilty. Bev liked to think she was only safeguarding her mother from hurt, but was that the truth? She was also protecting herself from the scrutiny of others. When people spoke badly of her mother, she felt it reflected on her parallel relationship with Dale.

Maybe Dale was right. Falling in love, or whatever the emotion was that she felt, had its difficult moments. It had roused fears, caused confusion and now provoked humiliation. Life wasn't fair.

Macy, her beautician, headed Bev's way and lifted the hood of the dryer. She tested a curl and deemed it dry. As Bev rose from under the hood and the church women realized her identity, they cringed before sending her an uncomfortable smile.

Bev managed a pleasant look but turned away without speaking to them. She had to weigh what she'd heard and decide if she should tell her mother. If these two women were talking about her, how many other people were having a romp with gossip?

Chapter Fourteen

Bev looked across the snow-covered hills as she settled onto the front of the toboggan. With Christmas only a couple of weeks away, she questioned her sanity coming along with Dale and the kids, but he'd promised he'd take them sledding, and here she was.

"You wait here," Dale said, his voice ringing in the stillness. "I want your mom and me to have a turn now."

Behind her, Michael and Kristin whined about the unfairness, but when she glanced over her shoulder, she saw Dale speaking to them in a softer voice she couldn't hear. When they smiled, Bev figured he'd worked his wiles on them.

The stress of the past weeks ebbed away as she breathed in the crisp air. The sun glazed the surrounding landscape, making it look like a wedding gown covered with beads and sequins. The snow sparkled and glinted, almost hurting her eyes while the picture triggered a hope for her future. She prayed Dale would soon ask her to marry him. She was ready.

The toboggan shifted as Dale moved it near the crest, and she felt him climb aboard, cuddling her. He wrapped his arms around her bulky jacket and planted a cold kiss on the nape of her neck. Bev let out a screech, then a chuckle as Dale nuzzled deeper.

"Aren't you going down?" Michael asked, apparently impatient with their antics.

"Give us a shove," Dale said.

The sled jerked, and she heard the children's laughter behind her as they shoved against Dale's back to slide the toboggan forward. As the sled left the crest, Bev looked back and saw the kids tumble to the ground, giggling.

Dale hugged her tightly when the sled bounded forward. The toboggan picked up speed and, skidding over a snowdrift, they became airborne before smacking to the ground. When they landed, the sled tilted, and Bev felt Dale slip from behind her on the sled.

Her error was to look behind her. As she turned, Bev lost her balance and tumbled from the board and slid the final distance on her bottom.

Bev sat in the cold snow, making sure her limbs were intact and grinning at her stupid mistake. The children's gleeful cries grew nearer as Dale pulled her from the ground. She brushed the snow from her backside as Michael raced up to her with a look of concern.

"I'm okay." She smiled so he'd believe her.

"Some ride," Dale said.

"I prefer riding down the hill all the way on the toboggan," Bev said.

Dale's eyes sparkled like the snow with mischief. Even though their parents' friendship had met problems, Dale had become more relaxed in the past weeks, as if his personal struggles had finally been resolved. Bev had to admit he'd kept his promise and had proven himself by doting on the children. The toboggan trip was an example.

"Let's go again," Michael called, already heading back up the hill.

"I'm through," Bev whispered so as not to disappoint the kids.

"Michael, you and Kristin go back up. I'll be there in a minute," Dale called. He took a step toward Bev, and then had second thoughts. He cupped his hand around his mouth and yelled. "Don't come down on the toboggan alone. Do you hear me?"

The children glanced over their shoulder, their faces crumpled with disappointment, but they finally gave a nod. Bev watched until they reached the top, then sighed, relieved, as she noticed them gathering snow into snowballs.

"I'm going to the car for the hot chocolate Mom sent along," Bev said. "We can have it when you come down."

Dale glanced up the hill. "I'll walk with you and

catch my breath. We can keep an eye on the kids from there."

Bev had laughed when her mother had supplied her with a large thermos of hot chocolate, some homemade cookies and a first-aid kit for their tobogganing trip. Her mother's paradoxical view was typical—ready for fun, yet prepared for an emergency.

Though she'd laughed at her mother's thoughtfulness, it also broke her heart. She was certain her mom's kindness had been partially generated by boredom. Following the gossip that had finally reached her ears, Mildred had avoided seeing Al for the past couple of weeks. The situation had turned into a standoff between the two dear friends.

Bev strode beside Dale, feeling his hand on hers, and in that private moment, she decided to ask the question she'd wanted to ask without the children hearing. "How's your Dad doing?"

He gave her a sidelong glance. "Terrible."

Her chest tightened. "Mom, too. Here we are having fun, and they're miserable. I can't get it out of my mind."

Dale released her hand when they reached the car, hit the remote and opened the back door. "Dad wouldn't go to church last week. I suppose you noticed."

She'd missed Al at the service but hadn't had the heart to ask. "Mom went to Unity Church. It's closer to her apartment she said. I'm afraid she's avoiding Fellowship Church like the plague."

Bev pulled out her mother's large thermos and grabbed four cups. Dale took them from her, then captured her free hand again and brought it to his lips. He held it there as if his kiss had set him thinking.

"I wonder if you should tell your mother that Dad isn't doing well."

"You think so?" At this point, Bev wanted to stay out of the situation. "I'm hoping that now she'll be so busy settling into her new apartment that maybe—"

"Christmas will be here in a couple of weeks," Dale interrupted, "and I can't handle this during the holidays. Church. Dinner. Nothing will be right. Who will I spend my Christmas with? My dad or you and the kids?"

Bev leaned against the car and let the question bang around in her head until she had another question of her own. "What about after the holidays, Dale? Are we going to complain if they continue seeing each other? We have to accept their decision. Either we're going to accept their friendship or we're not."

He nodded. "I'll accept whatever they decide."

"Right, and if we hear gossip, we'll have to squelch it or let it pass. We can't be hot and cold in this situation. It's too hurtful for them both."

He brushed the back of his hand against her cheek. "You're right. Let your mom know Dad's miserable. I can't watch him mope. This isn't like him."

He took Bev's hand and started back toward the hill. "Dad used to love his work. Now I hear it in his voice.

He's like a robot. Dad's always been filled with stories about people. Now? Nothing. It's as if he died with my mother."

"He did in a way."

"Well, it's got to stop. I don't want to lose both parents."

"I'll talk with Mom, but I can't promise anything."

"I know, but we'll pray. God will see the right thing happens."

Hearing Dale give the problem to God warmed her more than the hot chocolate would. He'd become a different man from the one she'd met in the parking lot the spring before.

"I'd better get up there before the kids do something we're sorry for," Dale said.

Bev slipped her arm around his shoulder and kissed his cheek. "Thanks, and I'll be waiting here with the hot chocolate."

With Bev's kiss still warming his cheek, Dale trudged up the hill, his feet sinking into the ankle-deep snow.

"Finally," Michael said in his pouty way. "We waited forever."

"It just felt like it, pal," Dale said, patting the boy's shoulder.

"Let's get going," Kristin said, dancing a jig around his legs. "I'm tired of waiting."

"Patience, young lady." Dale gave Kristin's ponytail a playful yank.

She spun around and jerked her hair away from him. "You're supposed to be nice."

"I am nice. I brought you sledding, didn't I?"

She grinned and tripped over her boot, then plopped into the snow. Dale chuckled and helped her to her feet.

"Let's get going," he said, positioning the sled at the crest of the hill. "Okay, all aboard."

"Can't I go down alone?" Michael asked.

"I don't think so, Michael. You have to steer this thing."

"I know how. I can do it," Michael said. He put his hand on his hip. "I'm not a baby."

Kristin pressed her fist on her hip. "I'm not a baby either."

"No, but you're a girl," Michael said.

Dale stepped in before the battle began. "And a mighty pretty girl, too."

He pondered the wisdom of allowing Michael to handle the smaller sled alone. It would give him a sense of accomplishment and be a positive stroke he needed if—

"Come on, Dale," Michael moaned. "Just this once."

"Only if you stop whining," Dale said, immediately sensing he'd made a mistake.

"Yippee!" Michael bellowed. He jumped around in circles like an athlete who scored the winning goal.

"Get on the sled, princess," Dale said to Kristin. "I'm honored to take a ride with the prettiest girl on the hill."

"I'm the only girl," she said, wrinkling her nose.

He chucked her under the chin, swept her into the air and plopped her on the front of the larger sled. He then pulled their toboggan to the crest of the hill. After he'd helped situate Michael, Dale stood behind his sled. "Ready?"

"Ready," Michael said.

"Let's go." Dale gave a running push and jumped onto his sled as it began its wild descent down the hill. Dale's toboggan moved ahead and he glanced back and saw Michael's sled not far behind. The children's screams of laughter filled his ears as Michael tore past.

But fear gripped Dale when he saw Michael hit a snowdrift and lose his balance. The toboggan seemed to ride on its side, and as it gained speed, he watched in horror as it flipped into the air, sending Michael tumbling down the hill in front of them.

While his heart thudded, Dale struggled to veer his toboggan away from Michael and his upturned sled. As they passed, Dale caught a glimpse of the boy and feared he'd been hurt.

Before Dale could climb from the toboggan, Bev had rushed to Michael's side. When Dale arrived, slowed by the snowdrifts, she sat on the ground cradling her son in her arms while blood ran from a gash in his forehead.

Dale crouched down, his stomach in knots, his guilt descending like a tornado. The incident had been his fault.

"He's okay," Bev said, "but the toboggan caught him in the head."

"I didn't mean to do it," Michael said, rubbing his brow near the spot where he'd been struck.

"Don't touch it," Bev said. "You'll get blood on your hands."

"It wasn't your fault, pal," Dale said, feeling the brunt of his stupidity. "I let you come down alone."

"It's okay, Dale. We all make mistakes." Bev leaned over and kissed Michael's head.

But it wasn't okay, and Dale knew it. He was the adult, the father figure who was wise yet fair. He should have said no instead of trying to make Michael happy.

While defeat settled over him, Dale pulled out his handkerchief and pressed it against Michael's wound.

"I'm okay," Michael said again, "and it was so much fun." He wriggled from his mother's arms and tried to stand. Instead, he plopped back onto the snow until Dale hoisted him off the ground and supported him until he had his balance.

"I can carry you back to the car," Dale said, ready to lift the boy.

"No, I can walk." Michael looked at Dale with pride, and despite his frustration with himself, Dale knew he'd given the boy one thing he needed—a sense of accomplishment.

But Dale had also learned one horrible truth. He was never cut out to be a father. He had too much to learn.

Bev hurried ahead across the white expanse toward the car, dragging the larger toboggan. "You laughed about my mother's first-aid kit," she called over her shoulder.

Kristin hovered at their side as Dale walked with Michael, one hand on his shoulder, the other pulling the smaller sled. He longed to hold the boy in his arms, to waylay his own fears that Michael might have been seriously injured. The day on the pier charged through his thoughts. The world was full of danger, and a father needed to be on guard. Dale's dad had been, and Dale should have been also.

He monitored his emotion for the sake of the children, and by the time they'd all plodded to the car, Bev had a bandage and disinfectant ready. While she worked on the wound, Dale loaded the toboggans, sorry that the day had ended on such a sad note and distraught over his glaring misjudgment.

When Bev had settled the kids into the car, she rounded to the trunk. "Dale, don't beat yourself up for this. You've been wonderful."

"I was stupid."

"No. You're like any parent, any person raising children. You give my kids love and attention. You spoil them—so unlike their own father. He loved them, but they didn't come first. His own interests did." She grasped his sleeve and forced him to look into her eyes. "It's different now. You've made the kids believe they're the most important people in the world in your eyes."

And they'd become that. Michael, Kristin and Bev

gave his life purpose and joy, but not if he couldn't meet the challenge. The old fear of commitment rose like a dragon, its fiery flames searing Dale's confidence and making him question the future again.

Christmas arrived in a flurry. Bev's spirit had lifted when her mother and Al had mended their relationship. When Mildred had heard that Al was depressed, she'd made the first move, and they decided to be more discreet. Though Bev understood and agreed, she felt saddened watching her mother and Al sneak around like teenagers hiding a new friend from their parents.

The saddest realization followed Michael's tobogganing accident. Dale hadn't been the same. Bev sensed it deep in her bones. Although he was attentive and thoughtful, his spirit had suffered the blow of his poor judgment. Bev wondered if Dale thought she'd never made a mistake with the children. He knew better. He'd seen her when they'd first met, frustrated and out of control, but she'd mellowed. She'd listened to Dale's wisdom and realized she'd missed the obvious while wallowing in her self-sacrifice. Michael needed special attention. He needed a father.

Christmas Day seemed to vanish before her eyes. Though Dale kept his mouth closed, she sensed he wanted to cry out to the heavens at the injustice of his mother's death. To add to the problem, Mildred had insisted on cooking dinner in Dotty's kitchen, and though Bev understood the reason, she saw that Dale resented it.

Al seemed to cope with the day. Occasionally his face took on a grave look, and Bev knew his thoughts were with Dotty. But most of the time he played with the children and reminisced about the good old days with her mother.

While Bev worked in the kitchen finishing up the last of the dishes, Dale wandered in and stood in the doorway. He leaned against the jamb, so unlike him lately. She'd begun to enjoy his surprise hugs and the kisses on the neck that sent shivers down her spine, but today he only stood and watched her.

"How's it going?" she asked, knowing it wasn't going well at all.

He shrugged and wandered closer, leaning his back against the counter. "I miss my mother."

Bev dropped the dish towel near the sink and shifted to his side. "Holidays are the worst."

Dale nodded and nibbled on the corner of his finger as if he had a hangnail. "I don't want to beat this to death, but we could have had our regular Christmas tree with all my mom's ornaments. That wasn't too much to ask." He paused and turned to Bev. "Or is it?"

She closed her eyes, drawing in strength to respond. His question put her in a position between Dale and her mother, a spot she didn't want to be in. "You know it's not too much. I suppose no one asked you."

Bev pictured the small Christmas tree in the Levins' living room, decorated with bows, draped ribbon and gold poinsettias—pretty, but her mother's idea, Bev knew. "Mom thought the regular decorations would be too much of an emotional reminder of your mom."

"Why does she want to keep my mother out of our holiday? She was part of my life since I was born. Couldn't we keep her traditions one more year?"

"Dale, you're asking the wrong person. I agree with you. My mom was trying to be kind, but she should have considered that you and your dad could decide what you could handle."

Dale lifted his hand and ran it across the back of his neck, then turned to her with such a sad expression, it broke her heart.

"I'm sorry, Bev," he said, sliding his arm around her waist and drawing her closer. "I'm putting you in the middle. You've done nothing wrong. It's Christmas and I should be holding the mistletoe over your head and letting you know how much you mean to me."

"Who needs mistletoe?" she asked, praying the distraction would ease the tension.

Dale's face eased to a half smile, and his lips met hers, so soft and warm she melted in his arms. He drew back, his eyes searching hers as if he had things to say but couldn't find the right words.

A giggle sailed in from the hallway, and they spun around to see Michael and Kristin watching.

"Yuck," Michael said. "Mushy stuff. When are we opening presents?"

Kristin covered her mouth as if holding back her giggles.

Dale stepped back, but didn't let go of Bev's waist. "In a few minutes. Your mother and I are talking."

"That's not talking," Michael said. "That's kissing." He vanished from the doorway with Kristin on his heels. Bev could hear them telling Mildred and Al it was almost time to open the gifts, but there were no comments about the smooching.

"We shouldn't let the kids see us kissing," she said.

"Why not? They should know what love looks like."

Bev's heart skipped a beat. Love. He'd never said the word before, not even in that context. She'd waited so long to hear him say he loved her. He still hadn't, but he'd gotten closer. She'd settle for that.

Chapter Fifteen

Dale felt angry at himself. Why had he allowed his emotions to surface on Christmas Day? He'd struggled to keep back his anger and his frustration with himself.

Love. He'd heard the word fly from his mouth without realizing it. He'd been so close to making a commitment, so ready to pry the rising words of love from his heart and tell Bev how she made his life whole and completed him in every way. But in the past two weeks, he'd felt as if he'd been thrown off a cliff.

Bev finally came in from the kitchen. They gathered around the tree with their gifts piled in front of them. Naturally, the children had the largest stacks, and Dale suggested they open theirs first. Electronic race-car games, a doll with a full wardrobe plus a sports car, books, puzzles and new clothing spread around their feet. Dale knew they couldn't keep track of who gave them what.

Bev opened hers next, sniffing the perfume, admiring the gold necklace and charm and modeling the new sweater. Dale followed, then his father, each pleased with the surprises found beneath the wrappings.

Mildred seemed delighted with the teapot that Bev had helped Dale select. It was a square pot, decorated with a dark background and a myriad of tiny flowers. Chintz, Bev had called it. English china. Dale knew nothing about teapots, but he knew Mildred was pleased.

Finally Al set a package onto Mildred's lap. The box was small, and Dale felt his blood pressure rise. He couldn't imagine that his father would give Mildred what he feared.

Mildred eyed the package and gave Al a wary look, but his father only smiled. She pulled the paper from the dark blue box and lifted the lid. Without speaking, her gaze shifted from the gift to Al and back again.

"What is this, Al?" Mildred asked, reaching into the box and lifting a gold chain with a pendant that blinked with diamonds.

"It was Dotty's," Al said. "I don't have a daughter, and I doubt Dale would want to wear it."

He sent Dale a smile, and Dale did all he could not to rebel. His father didn't seem to notice.

"Dotty had so much jewelry she'd gathered through the years," Al said. "I have plenty for Dale's wife—if he ever marries, that is." He gave Dale a raised eyebrow.

Dale sank into the cushion. His father was right. He wouldn't use the jewelry, but it had been his mother's. How could his dad give it away to a friend? He glanced at Bev and saw her distress, but in a heartbeat, she shifted her gaze to the necklace.

"It's beautiful," she said. She kept her eyes averted as if afraid to see the look on Dale's face.

"I shouldn't accept this," Mildred said, "but I'm touched that you want me to have it."

"You loved Dotty, too." Al rose, then took the chain from her hands and opened the clasp.

Mildred shifted her hair while Al placed it around her neck and stood back. "Jewelry needs to be worn. It's lifeless in a box."

So was his mother, Dale thought, swallowing the hurt he felt. Shame washed over him. He knew he was being obstinate, but he couldn't help the feelings that roiled within him. If things kept up the way they were, he couldn't see how he and Bev would ever make a go of their relationship. How could he resent her mother and still be civil? Blood was thicker than water, he knew. Resenting her mother and failure as a father-figure left little promise in Dale's eyes. Commitment was a laugh. He wondered how he'd even thought it possible.

"And here's my next surprise," his father said. "I've decided to retire after inventory in January. I'll keep the drugstore, hire a full-time pharmacist and a store manager. I want to enjoy my life. At least, what I have left of it. I want to travel and spend time with the people I love."

Dale rose and began to gather the torn pieces of wrapping paper and smashed bows, feeling crushed by his father's news. He busied himself cleaning the floor while the others offered their congratulations to his father.

Unable to deal with his hurt, Dale hurried from the room, pulled a trash bag from the closet and stuffed the debris into it. His fist jammed the Christmas paper and colorful ribbon into a wad while he wished he could minimize his feelings as easily.

So much for devotion.

He controlled himself through dessert and the rest of the evening. Bev had gotten quieter, too. He didn't know if she realized he was upset or if she felt the same. He'd talk to her later, but something had to give.

When the others had gone home and he and his father were alone, Dale finally spoke. "So you're really doing it?"

His father lifted his head from admiring the cardigan he'd received from Mildred and placed it in his lap. "You mean retiring?"

Dale nodded.

"We talked about this before, Dale. It's the right thing for me to do. I'm not concentrating at the pharmacy, and I could make a mistake. I've lost my spirit there."

"But why? I still don't get it. If you'd retired while Mom was alive, I'd understand. What are you going to do with yourself?"

"I already told you. Travel, laugh, enjoy whatever life I still have. I'm going to live."

He glared at his father, disbelieving. His father was only sixty. He could work for years.

Al folded the sweater and placed it back in the box by his feet. "Since your mother died, I've come to realize how precious life is. I see how we waste it on unimportant things. I'm not going to do that anymore." His eyes misted.

"You know, Dale…" His father leaned forward and dropped his face into his hands. He rubbed at his eyes, forever it seemed, until he looked up. "It's finally hit me, Son."

Dale felt his chest tighten and fear coursed through him. He felt certain from the look on his father's face that he didn't want to hear what he had to say.

"I'm ashamed to tell you this, but I needed to work these past years to get away from your mother's illness. I pray the good Lord doesn't put you in that situation, having to watch your wife die. I've finally been able to face how horrible it was."

He shook his head and looked at Dale. "I loved your mother more than any other woman, but I needed to work. Sitting there day in, day out surrounded by sadness and sickness without a reprieve kills the spirit."

Dale rose and walked to the window. "You're right, Dad, I don't want to hear this."

"But you should. I know you resent Millie, but she

saved us in a way. Saved your mother and me from de-
pression. We were so bound in our sorrow we'd almost
stopped talking. Millie came along and brought life
back into our house. For your mother and me both. It
was the first time I'd heard Dotty laugh in months. Do
you know what that did for my heart? It made it sing."

Dale spun around, his body rigid. "You gave her
Mom's diamond pendant." Distress prickled down his
limbs. "How could you do that?"

"It was easy, Dale. Your mom's not going to wear that
jewelry anymore. She doesn't need it. She's in glory,
Son. She's glowing in heaven with the angels, all fresh
and healthy. And like I said, jewelry needs to be worn.
It's lifeless in a box."

Dale opened his mouth and closed it, overwhelmed
by his feelings of resentment.

"And so am I, Son. If I box myself away from the
world and wallow in grief, I'm lifeless, too. Do you want
me to do that?"

Dale felt tears press behind his eyes. He looked into
his father's strained face and went to him. "I'm sorry,
Dad," he whispered.

"I know."

Dale felt like a child wrapped in his father's strong
arms. Where was his strength and support for his father?
Tears welled in Dale's eyes and rolled down his cheeks,
and he felt his father's shoulders shudder with his own
sorrow.

The Christmas-tree lights blurred and ran together while they embraced, releasing the grief they'd contained for too long.

Since Christmas, Dale slipped into silence. Bev knew that something had happened, but she had no idea what unless it was the constant stress about her mother's relationship with Al. Sometimes Dale was like a boy with a secret. His behavior taunted her, and she longed to know what was on his mind. But Dale had a way of shutting people out. She could only pray it had nothing to do with her or the children.

Her mother and Al had continued their cloaked friendship, avoiding public places for fear of gossip. Her mother continued attending Unity Church while Al had returned to Fellowship. The whole situation broke Bev's heart, and she felt as if she were part of the problem. She'd told her mother about the gossip at the beauty salon and nagged at her about what her and Al's friendship might look like to others. Much of her fear was that the relationship would scare away Dale. Her own selfish purpose, she admitted.

Outside she heard Dale's car pull into the driveway to pick them up for Sunday-morning worship, and the children came out of their rooms, Kristin tying her shoe while trying to walk.

When she opened the door, Bev felt disappointment that Dale no longer gave her a kiss on her cheek. Her gaze drifted toward his empty car in the driveway. "Where's your dad?"

"He said he'd meet us there." Dale picked up Michael's jacket from a nearby chair and held it out for him.

Bev bundled Kristin into her warm coat, and they stepped outside into the mid-January cold to hurry into Dale's pre-warmed car. Bev had grown to love the feeling of family, and she'd begun to realize she was ready to accept the commitment of marriage. She glanced at her two children and then at Dale, letting her dreams flow. One day she might hold a new baby in her arms— another child to love.

Dale shifted into Reverse and pushed the button on the radio. Praise music filled the car as they drove, leaving little room for conversation. When the church's steeple came into view, Bev was comforted that God was looking down on them.

Kristin hurried off to Sunday school, but Michael lingered behind, wanting to stay in church. Bev knew he only wanted to stay glued to Dale, so she scooted him off and made him promise to stay there.

Dale clasped her arm as they climbed the steps into the building. The scent of polished wood greeted her as she made her way into the sanctuary. When they headed down the aisle, Bev froze.

She saw her mother near the front, her head pivoted as if looking for her. Bev felt Dale cringe at her side, and she feared looking at him. She prayed that he would accept the inevitable, but he had not resolved what seemed to be the Lord's will. Bev's heart sank, knowing her relationship with Dale might never be the same.

When her mother noticed them, a smile lit her face. Al sat beside her. For some reason, they'd obviously changed their minds about being low-key, and Bev could almost hear a buzz as people watched them together. Her mother and Al smiled at each other with a comfort and familiarity that only came from knowing someone deeply.

Bev wasn't worried about her mother's indiscretion. She was confident in her mother's Christian morals, but did the others know her that well?

Mildred beckoned, and Bev and Dale continued down the aisle until they reached the pew. Bev slid in first and Dale followed. She eyed her mother, wanting so much to ask why she'd changed her mind.

As if her mother knew what she was thinking, Mildred rested her hand on Bev's and gave it a pat. "We've discussed this with the pastor, and we're following his suggestion," she whispered.

We've discussed this with the pastor? Her mother's comment sent Bev's heart reeling. They'd discussed exactly what with the pastor? But this wasn't the time to question. Bev bowed her head, asking the Lord to help her focus on His Word, not on the thoughts and attitudes of those around her.

She raised her head, her fears covered by the strength that she'd received from her earnest prayers and from an amazing new sense that God had heard her prayer.

When the pastor rose for the sermon, Mildred gave her hand a pat, and Bev noticed that her other hand rested on Al's. She looked content, and whatever happened, whatever the pastor had said to them, Bev knew God was in charge.

The pastor paused with his Bible open. His gaze traveled over the length of the congregation. "Our reading today is from 2 Thessalonians 3:11-18. I challenge you to listen to Paul's words to the people of Thessaly. 'We hear that some among you are idle. They are not busy; they are busybodies. Such people we command and urge in the Lord Jesus Christ to settle down and earn the bread they eat. And as for you, brothers, never tire of doing what is right. If anyone does not obey our instruction in this letter, take special note of him. Do not associate with him, in order that he may feel ashamed. Yet do not regard him as an enemy, but warn him as a brother.'"

Bev gave a sidelong glance at her mother and saw her smile. As the pastor continued to expound on the dangers of gossip, her mother's focus didn't waver.

The pastor's voice rose. "And as Paul said in conclusion, 'Now may the Lord of peace himself give you peace at all times and in every way. The Lord be with all of you. These are my words to you. Go in peace and remember that your attitude should be as that of Jesus Christ.'"

But when she looked toward Dale, his expression hadn't changed. He sat as if he hadn't heard or understood the pastor's message.

Music filled the church, and the congregation stood, lifting their voices in song. Bev tried to push aside Dale's attitude and sing from her heart, feeling strength in God's mercy and love.

When the last hymn faded, Dale bolted toward the door, leaving Bev confused. She hurried after him, but came to a halt when Rod Drake, one of the church deacons, came up behind Dale and grasped his shoulder.

"How are things?" he asked with a quirky smile.

"I see you have a friendly little family gathering today."

"Right," Dale said.

Rod grinned as his eyes shifted toward her mother and Al making their way to the back of the church. "Looks like one of these days you'll find yourself becoming your own grandpaw." He delivered the line with a singsong twang, then gave Dale's arm a playful punch.

Bev opened her mouth, but then closed it and pulled on Dale's arm. "We need to go," she said. Before she could move, Dale pushed past her and hurried toward the door.

Fear charged through her limbs as she fled down the stairs toward the parking lot. "Dale," she called.

He stopped and turned toward Bev. His face was twisted with resentment and anger, and she knew she could say nothing to make things better.

"I can't cope with all the innuendos and jokes, Bev. I'm sorry. I don't know why this bothers me, but it does. Until we can get this settled—"

"Until *you* can get it settled," Bev said, her frustration surfacing. She felt her world coming to a screeching halt.

"Okay, until *I* can get it settled. I don't want to be the laughingstock of Loving or anywhere."

Her arms hung at her sides in disbelief. He hadn't listened to the pastor's sermon. What could she say? She couldn't rationalize this with him no matter what she said. They'd been through it before. Dale had issues he needed to deal with, and she couldn't do it for him.

"Are you coming?" he asked.

"No. You go ahead." She clamped her teeth tightly, her cheek ticking with frustration and anger.

He frowned. "How will you get home?"

"I have friends. My mom. Anyone but you, Dale. Go home and think this over. If you ever resolve all of your problems, if you can think of someone else other than yourself, then you can let me know—if I even care by then."

He stood like a statue, his mouth drooping, his beautiful eyes shadowed. "Bev, please—"

"Forget it, Dale. I can't deal with it anymore either."

Chapter Sixteen

On Sunday afternoon, Dale sat at his father's, feeling the sting of Bev's anger. Her bitter rejection had forced him to face the truth. His problem didn't stem from one issue, but multiple stressful situations he'd dealt with recently. Yet it all boiled down to commitment. He'd talked himself in and out of his feelings for Bev from the moment he realized he was falling for her.

He couldn't talk himself out of it anymore. He loved Bev, and to his amazement, he adored the children. He'd had no idea how protective siblings could be, nor had he understood what fun and camaraderie siblings could share. He'd never experienced it. Dale realized he'd missed out on a wonderful experience.

Since he'd gotten home from church and his father had gone to the pharmacy to work on the year-end inventory, he'd sat alone asking himself how he could go back to Grand Rapids without resolving the dreadful parting with Bev. He couldn't live with himself if he didn't. Numerous times he'd headed for the telephone then walked away, fearing she would reject him again.

Had he been wrong today? Should he have laughed off Rod Drake's ignorant comment? The same thought had crossed his mind as he'd watched his father grow closer and closer to Mildred. What had happened to devotion? What had happened to his father's soul mate? What had happened to his own faith in the perfect marriage?

What difference did it make? He'd resolved to stay single, to live alone and enjoy the freedom. Funny thing, since meeting Bev and the kids, he'd learned the difference between being alone and being lonely. Without them, the apartment he'd called home felt empty. His nights felt lonely. He'd never experienced those raw feelings before Bev came into his life.

Stand firm in the faith; be men of courage; be strong. Do everything in love. Like a bolt of lightning, the Scripture tore through his mind. Dale had begun to read God's Word and it had given him strength, but in recent weeks he'd failed. He was not a man of courage. He wasn't strong, and he'd drifted so far from love he felt like a shipwrecked man without a life jacket.

Courage. The word caused him to rise. If God had truly brought him and Bev together for a purpose, and he'd believed it was so, he couldn't give up without a fight. He charged to the telephone, grasped the receiver and punched in her phone number.

Bev caved into the sofa cushion and lowered her face into her hands. She'd agreed to see Dale against her better judgment. Why drag on a relationship that had nowhere to go?

She'd truly believed that God had been involved in their friendship. The silly grocery-store incident, the coincidence of her mother knowing Al, her mom being caregiver to Dotty, being members of the same church. The list could go on and on. Once she'd speculated that perhaps God was leading her mother toward Dotty's care and the meeting had nothing to do with Dale. Could that have been the only reason? The thought hurt in the pit of her stomach.

Saying no to Dale's request could have been easier had Bev not had her own confession to make. Today she felt it only fair to tell Dale the truth about her past. Perhaps he could understand why she'd been so afraid of falling in love when she'd met him.

Her mother had invited the children to the movies. Now that Dale had called, Bev was grateful they weren't home.

A car door slammed, causing her to jump. She grasped her emotions and pulled them together. She needed to stand firm on her convictions. Dale had meant everything to her, but she feared he would never change.

The doorbell rang, and Bev moved to the door unable to smile. When she opened it, Dale stood on the other side, his generous smile gone, his full lips pinched with distress.

She pushed open the storm door and he stepped inside, bringing in the winter's cold.

He stood in the foyer as if not knowing where to go.

Bev swung her arm toward the living room, then closed the door behind him as he wandered ahead of her seemingly in a daze.

"We don't have too long before the kids are back, so let's get this over with," she said, surprised at the anger that still radiated in her tone.

Dale looked surprised, then hurt. He still wore his jacket, and he scrunched down in the chair like a lost man. "I don't know where to begin, Bev. Today felt like a stab. I thought I was dealing with our folks' friendship, but I can't seem to shake my feelings."

What could she say that she hadn't said before? Bev felt her arms flail with hopelessness. "Did you listen to the sermon? I don't think you did."

"I heard it, but our issue wasn't gossip. It was—I guess I feel betrayed."

"Betrayed? By me?" Her shoulders stiffened.

"No. By my father."

His response rocked her backward. "Why? Because of my mother? It's a friendship, Dale. Can't you see that?"

"I always thought my dad adored my mother just like I knew he thought I was the greatest son in the world. I was the center of their lives. But after my mom died, I don't know, he seemed to step right up beside Mildred and forget my mother. I resent that."

"It's not forgetting your mother, Dale."

His head shot upward, and she saw in his face he didn't understand. "You believed he'd forgotten you."

Dale blanched. She'd startled him.

"That's not it," he said, but he didn't sound convincing. "I realize your mother walked in at a time when she was needed. Remember, I wanted someone to give Dad some assistance. Dad said my mother and he had stopped talking. They couldn't face the inevitable, so they just went through the motions of living until Mildred appeared on the scene."

"Then you should be grateful, not angry."

"I'm not angry."

"If it's not anger, why do you feel betrayed? You need to sort out your feelings. You can't find the reason for an emotion when you're looking at the wrong one. Are you angry or are you hurt?"

"Hurt? Why would I be hurt?"

Bev drew up her shoulders, not believing that Dale could hide the truth from himself. "You're a good son, Dale. Think of the fourth commandment. You've followed it to the letter—honor your father and mother, speak well of them, respect them. You've done it all."

Dale winced. "I wanted to do more. Adult children

don't see their parents with adult eyes sometimes. I finally figured that out."

Bev was struck by what he said. She'd struggled herself with her relationship to her mother. She'd wanted her mother's full attention when she'd moved in, she'd encouraged her to care for Dotty, then had resented it. She'd felt the same way Dale did.

"I was still looking at myself as my parents' child," Dale said. "I didn't want to see their flaws. I couldn't handle their humanness. I couldn't bear to see my father happy after my mother died. I wanted him to be grief-stricken. Then I could come in as the hero-son and make his life better. But that didn't happen. Your mother walked in and took over. I resented that."

Bev thought of confessing her similar feelings, but not tonight. She had other issues and her own confession to make. She leaned nearer, riveting her gaze to his. "God looks in your heart. He knows your struggles. All you had to do was give it up, and let the Lord bless you for standing by their side and loving them."

He gave a thoughtful nod, looking distracted. "I realized something else today. My mom and dad doted on me, but I missed out on something because of it. I was the little king. Very self-absorbed. I didn't like to share things." He halted a moment. "Things or people."

"Doesn't that explain why you've resented my mother's friendship with your dad?"

He didn't respond, and Bev had no idea if he were

listening, but she had no plan to stop. Today she wanted to wipe the slate clean, if not for herself for him. Dale would never be happy until he discovered who he was.

"I know my kids have been a problem for you," she said, "but you've resolved it. I'm proud of you for that, but I think you've beaten yourself up over making one error in judgment. I said this before, Dale. I'm not a perfect parent either. I make my share of mistakes, but you know what?"

Her question captured his attention. Finally he looked directly into her eyes.

"We make mistakes out of love. We love someone so much that we want to please them, and sometimes in trying to be everything to our kids, wives, husbands or even parents, we do them a disservice. Please, think about that. Love isn't the problem, Dale. It's the answer."

Dale shifted forward and rested his face in his hands as if defeated. Bev wanted to stop, to let him go, to say goodbye, but that was her head's reaction. Her heart wanted to hold him and share his tears. He was hurting.

"I'd better go," he said, rising so quickly he surprised her. "I thought I had more to say, but you're right. I need to ask myself some questions."

She stepped forward and caught his arm. "Please, wait a moment. Give me a turn."

His dismal expression flickered with confusion. "Your turn?"

"My turn." She gestured toward the chair.

He glanced at it but didn't move, as if he were calculating whether to stay.

Bev's chest tightened around her heart, knowing what she would confess, her secret that she'd never told a soul, but she owed it to Dale so he could understand.

Finally he backed up and sat, his spine rigid, his fingers knotted together, his jaw twitching.

"I have something important to tell you." She'd caught a flicker of concern in his eyes as he studied her face.

"Something serious?" he asked.

"It is to me." Her gaze drifted to the hazy sun coming through the window, capturing her silhouette. Reflections could never expose the internal struggle within anyone. "It's a confession."

"Confession?" His head tilted as his eyes searched hers.

"I want to clarify some things about my marriage." Bev drew in a lengthy breath, hoping she could find the right words. "I tend to blame Jesse for the mess we were in, but I was as much at fault. I made a lot of mistakes, too, Dale. I thought if I told you, you could more fully understand the fear I've felt about getting involved again."

"Tell me. Please." His back relaxed and he leaned forward.

Bev licked her lips to moisten them. Panic raced through her, and her hands trembled.

"I've blamed Jesse for our less-than-perfect marriage, but it goes two ways. He rode motorcycles when we met. I rode on the bike with him, enjoying the wind in my hair and the freedom. I was young and away from family for the first time. But things changed when we had the kids. I expected Jesse to change, too. I called him selfish and self-centered, and he was, but it was no surprise. I'd made a bad choice."

As she spoke, disbelief struck Dale's face. She saw him struggle with her confession.

"But my greatest mistake was with the Lord. I made a vow until death us do part, and I wanted out of that commitment then. I didn't know death would come so fast and life would deal us a financial blow, but when Jesse died—" She paused and swallowed hard to lose the words that hung in her throat. "I felt relief as well as sadness. I'm ashamed of that."

Dale's eyes narrowed. In his gaze, she saw the dark storm she'd seen come and go with his own struggles.

"It's horrible to admit," she continued, "but I was relieved I didn't have to deal with my promise to God any longer. I didn't have to live as if I were the picture of happiness when I was miserable half the time. It's horrible that I felt that way, but it's taught me a vital lesson."

Dale had drawn back as if sorting through what she'd said, and Bev prayed that he would understand. She thought too much of him to let the memories of their good times together be tainted by her admission.

"Relationships aren't always perfect. Soul mates are created by God. They're not a human's decision, and that's why I hadn't been able to handle our friendship better than I did. Even though my heart told me one thing, I asked myself if I was really listening to God's direction, or was I making another mistake listening to my own need?"

"You weren't making a mistake this time, Bev," he said. "I would never make a commitment without knowing for sure I could handle it or knowing I would give it my all."

Bev's heart twisted. She realized that commitment was a problem with Dale. He feared it, and that's what made their relationship hopeless.

"I wanted you to know why I could never marry anyone who is self-centered or who's not strong and willing to be a real partner in the marriage. I need to feel confident in that. It's taken me a long time to allow myself to accept those feelings again."

Dale opened his mouth and closed it as if lost for words. The realization that they would never be a couple broke her heart. Despite this certainty, she longed to find she was wrong, but that would never be.

"Before you leave, I want to say thank you."

"Thank me? For what?" He looked at her in disbelief.

"Thank you for opening my eyes. One thing I learned from our friendship is that I can love again. I'm ready for marriage and ready to be a mother again. I might never have known that if you hadn't come along."

"Bev, I—"

She held up her hand. "I don't want any words of regret or empty promises. I just want to say goodbye as friends."

"Goodbye?"

She tore herself from the chair and aimed her blurred eyes toward the door. The last thing she wanted to do was let him see her cry.

"Bev…" His voice trailed off as he followed her to the open door, searching her face for something he wouldn't see.

"Goodbye, Dale." She pushed the opening wider, letting in the bitter cold that felt warmer than her heart.

He didn't say a word.

As he descended the stairs, the tears rose behind her eyes and pooled on her lashes. When his car left the driveway, it was only an obscure image.

A blurred shadow.

Remnants of rock salt still sparkled on the concrete walk of Dale's apartment. The low temperatures had halted any fresh snow, and now the white heaps had darkened to a dirty gray, about as soiled and despondent as Dale felt. He wrapped his jacket around him and bent his head to the cold wind.

Now, coming home from work, the loneliness seemed unbearable. In the past, he could pick up the phone and talk with Bev. In the background, he'd hear the kids jabbering about something. They always needed her as soon as she got on the telephone. Through his sadness, nostalgia made him grin.

He missed Bev more than he'd ever missed anyone. Even more than his mom, which seemed unbelievable. But he knew his mother was in heaven, healthy again and hanging around with all her loved ones who'd gone before. She was in the presence of the Lord, walking with Jesus in the garden, hearing the angel song. Bev was sitting in Loving. Missing him? He had no clue. Did the children miss him?

The ache stabbed through his heart. He missed Kristin's silly giggle and Michael's wide eyes watching everything he did. He'd become the child's hero, and Dale had allowed his own juvenile behavior, his fear of inadequacy, his unfounded apprehension of commitment to hold him back from the best thing that had happened to him.

In the past weeks, Dale had sorted through all that had held him back from Bev. He'd read the Bible over and over, passages that he'd learned to love. A verse from Ecclesiastes rolled across his thoughts like a soothing balm. *Two are better than one, because they have a good return for their work: If one falls down, his friend can help him up. But pity the man who falls and has no one to help him up! Also, if two lie down together, they will keep warm. But how can one keep warm alone?*

Tears rolled down Dale's cheeks as they had since he had walked out Bev's door. Who would keep him warm?

Who would pick him up when he fell? His earlier concerns seemed unimportant, bordering on the ridiculous.

Dale had spent many nights in prayer, asking God to forgive him. He'd tossed in the night, unable to sleep, still dressed from the day before because he'd wept himself to sleep. Shame flooded him.

He thought of his father, a man who understood that God had given him a friend to help him through his troubles. He'd resented Mildred who'd come to his family's aid, who'd given up her time to show her love to his parents—even to Dale.

Bev had been dragged into the situation with her own sorrow. She'd become Dale's friend, allowed her children to love him, stood strong in her faith and willingly gave her burdens to the Lord. She'd grown. Dale hadn't. Bev had opened her heart and laid her secret on the table. She'd admitted her weakness and had resolved it with the Lord and herself. Bev was ready for marriage.

Dale had been ready for nothing but self-pity.

How could the Lord forgive him for his distrust? God had promised to be with him, to help him ride the waves of fear and calm his storms, but Dale had plodded along caught up in his human dilemma and walked right past the Lord's open arms. *Do not be afraid, I am with you. I will bless you.* He'd read it in Genesis—the very beginning of the Bible. Dale knew he had read that promise over and over, but he'd rejected God's love offered to him with open arms.

And so had Bev's arms opened wide, but he'd smacked them away with his spoiled-rotten attitude. He'd promised her once that he'd learn to deal with her children. Dale had done more than that. He loved them. He'd also promised her that he'd never abandon her, yet he had.

Would she ever believe his promises again?

Dale lowered his head, holding back his incessant tears, and promised God to listen to his direction.

Dale knew he would keep this promise. The stakes were precious.

Chapter Seventeen

Bev heard a car door, and her heart skipped. She had prayed Dale would call since the day she sent him away, and he had. He'd invited her to dinner. When she glanced out the window and saw him, she lifted her eyes heavenward and whispered a thank-you.

She pulled open the door, and Dale stood on the porch with a different look in his eyes than she'd seen in months—determination, relief, love. Today she saw the same blue eyes she remembered so well, the gaze that dragged her into a whirlpool of longing and dreams.

She prayed that tonight would not be a dream, but a reality.

"Hi," Dale said through the storm door. He seemed more nervous than she did.

Bev pushed back the door and stepped aside.

He passed her and stepped through the archway. She

missed the embrace she'd grown to love, but she understood. He'd come to talk with her. She closed the door and followed him into the living room. "Are you okay?"

"No." He turned to face her. "How about you?"

She drew in a breath and gave an honest answer. "I'm miserable."

He opened his arms, and she stepped into his embrace without misgivings. His coat felt cold against her skin, but Bev didn't care. She drew in the familiar scent of his aftershave mingled with the crisp outside air, loving every icy moment, yet fearing it, too.

When he released her, he slipped off his topcoat and dropped it on the chair. He'd dressed in a navy pinstriped suit with a navy and burgundy tie. She'd never seen him so handsome, and she grasped the chair back to stem the emotion.

"The kids aren't here?" He glanced toward the hallway.

"They're with my mother for the evening. I thought it best. I didn't tell them you were coming." Her eyes captured his, and she spoke from the heart. "But I'm more than pleased you're here."

"Me, too." He drew her to his side, and they sat on the sofa facing each other. "I've missed you terribly. I never knew life could be so lonely."

"I've been lonely, too. When you walked away—"

"You sent me away," he said.

She shook her head. Bev remembered the day too well and, not just a day, the weeks he'd withdrawn.

Grasping for courage, she told him, detailing his coldness and reliving the hurt she felt.

Sorrow filled his eyes hooded by thick, dark lashes. "I've cried myself to sleep over you, Bev."

She brushed her hand along his jaw feeling his smooth fresh-shaven skin. "Tears never hurt anyone. They're healing." Touched by his honesty, she reached upward and kissed his cheek where she knew his tears had been.

Dale captured her face and cupped her cheek in his hand. He lowered his mouth to hers, his kiss as soft and tender as down. "I'm so sorry for the foolishness. I'm asking your forgiveness."

Bev's heart lurched at his request. She'd longed to hear those words months earlier. But concern still clung to her as she remembered his empty promises. "I forgive you, but it's hard to forget. I need to feel confident that you've come to some kind of resolution with—"

"I have. God is my witness." He raised his hand in an oath.

The certainty of his voice, and the reference to the Lord stopped Bev from questioning. "I'd like to hear it."

He studied her face, his eyes filled with apology and tenderness, and he told her the details of his struggle.

Holding her breath, Bev listened with her head and heart. She saw his sorrow, she felt his struggle and she witnessed his transformation.

"Thank you," Bev said when he finished. "I think we've both grown, and we've learned from each other."

Dale's strong arm drew her nearer. "You've even helped me find my faith. You've opened windows and doors for me, a whole world I didn't know before."

"You knew," she said. "You didn't trust yourself to take a step outside."

He caressed her jaw, her cheek, then leaned over to brush his lips across her eyes. "I can never thank you enough for that. I'm still weak in my renewed faith, but it's a beginning, and with your strength, I'll continue to grow."

Bev held her breath. His admission held promise. It gave her hope.

"Another thing I realized is how much I love your children. They mean the world to me, and so do you, Bev. I've missed you all so much."

Her pulse kicked. He loved her children, but did he love her? She wanted to hear him say it with all her heart. "Where do we go from here, Dale?"

He shifted and nestled her to his side. "We go right here in my arms."

His mouth touched hers, and the familiar pressure sent her reeling. They were flawed people who needed God badly. But Bev slowed her thoughts and melted into the kiss. Her fears faded while confidence unfurled. This time she knew they would make it. She'd prayed, and she believed God was on their side.

Dale's hands made gentle circles on her back while his lips caressed hers. When his fingers nestled in her hair, she trembled in his arms, and he answered with a quiet sigh before he released her.

"We're going to be all right," Bev said.

"More than all right."

He brushed his lips against her hand. "Before we leave for the restaurant, will you pray with me, Bev? We need to pray for our parents and for us. Our folks need our understanding and acceptance, and whatever they're led to do we have to deal with it."

Her heart lifted at his request. They joined hands, and she closed her eyes. He'd never said it, but Bev felt loved.

"Thank you for the wonderful evening," Bev said, looking out the wide window overlooking the Bay Breeze waterfront.

"You're welcome," Dale said, "but you don't have to thank me. You deserve every amazing moment."

Dale gazed out the window toward Lake Michigan. The trees scattered around the resort bent against a brisk February wind. Out on the lake, ice masses loomed at the shoreline, and the long pier and moorings looked shrouded in an icy coating, but Dale's heart felt like springtime.

Bev lifted her cup and took a sip of hot coffee. Her mind seemed miles away.

"Something wrong?" Her distraction cooled his warm thoughts.

"I'm fine. Just thinking about a lot of things."

"Thinking?"

"About us."

His pulse skipped, knowing she'd opened the door he'd been waiting for. "Me, too." He was grinning most of the time.

"Really?"

Her hair glinted in the flickering candlelight and left him breathless. "You're the most beautiful woman I know, Bev."

She lowered her gaze, as if disbelieving.

He reached across the tabletop and rested his hand over hers. "I'm telling the truth."

"Thank you," she said, without looking at him. "You're a handsome man yourself." She finally lifted her head, giving him a shy smile.

For a moment, he hesitated. The words he wanted to say clung to the roof of his mouth, but they needed saying. He'd waited far too long.

"I love you, Bev."

It seemed a moment before his words registered. When they did, her head bobbed up and her eyes searched his.

"I've loved you for so long. I had a difficult time admitting it. I almost felt unworthy of you."

Her head tilted back as if he'd flung a brick at her. "Unworthy? In what way?"

The truth came powering over him. "You had your head on straight. You'd raised two kids by yourself while

I was floundering. You always seemed together. I was falling apart."

"The operative word is *seemed* together." She grinned, sending his heart on a romp. "Look at the mess I sometimes make with the kids. We were blessed to have met."

"You're right about that," Dale said, thinking of all the ways they'd touched each other's lives. "I hope you knew that I loved you even though I never said it."

"I do now," she said. "And I love hearing it. I've waited forever." She reached across the table and touched his hand. "I love you, too."

They were wasting precious time. Dale captured her hand as he stood. "Let's get out of here. We have unfinished business."

He tossed money on the table beside the bill, helped Bev on with her coat and guided her to the exit. As they stepped outside, Dale maneuvered her into the shelter of the building and drew her against his chest. As his lips sought hers, he breathed in the crisp winter air and the heady scent of her fragrance. It surrounded him as sweetly as the love that wrapped around his heart.

He clasped her closer as his kiss lingered. Longing coursed through him, and his emotions mounted.

Bev trembled, and Dale drew back. "Let's get into the car. You're cold."

She lifted her gaze and shook her head. "I'm not cold."

He caught her meaning and felt a wry smile glide across his face. "Then we'd better stop."

In truth, Dale didn't want to stop, but respect and Christian morals told him otherwise. He grasped Bev's slender hand, then bent his head to the cold as he led her to the car, knowing that nothing could stand in their way anymore, not even the cold February wind.

Chapter Eighteen

$\sim$

Bev placed an Easter basket on the floor in front of each of the children. "Are you ready for the egg hunt?"

"Yeah," they both said, jumping up and running for their shoes.

"Hold on there," Al said, beckoning to the children.

They gave him a questioning look, then bounded to his side.

"What do candy and baskets have to do with Easter?" Al asked.

Kristin paused a moment, her face weighted with serious thought. "They're presents."

"But it's not Christmas," Al said. "Jesus's birth was God's present to us."

"So is Easter," Kristin said.

Al gave her a questioning look. "How?"

Kristin gave a frantic look toward Michael. "Because Jesus died for our sins and that's the best gift of all."

Al's face brightened, and applause filled the room at Kristin's explanation.

"What about you, Mr. Michael?" Al's question took Michael's look of relief and squelched it.

"Thought you got out of answering, didn't you?" Dale said, giving him a little poke with his toe.

"I know something else about Easter," Michael said.

"Lay it on us," Dale said.

"In Sunday school we learned that Easter is like the springtime when the dead things come to life again."

Dale's memory flew back to earlier thoughts. "That's it Michael. Rebirth."

The boy tilted his head and grinned. "That's what I meant."

"And that's what you said," Al added. "Being reborn. We all need it…in so many ways."

Bev's chest swelled at her son's response.

The children wavered a minute before Al chuckled and gave them a hug. "When you come back with those eggs, I might just have something to add to your do-bobs."

They charged out of the room, their baskets swinging from their hands.

Bev heard the back door slam, and she sank onto the sofa beside Dale. For the first time, she noticed her mother's apprehensive look and gave Dale a questioning poke.

He shrugged and folded his hands as Mildred slid to the edge of her chair.

"Speaking of being reborn—" Mildred gave Al a lengthy look, then shifted her focus back to Bev and Dale. "I know both of you have struggled with Al's and my relationship." She paused, letting her comment settle in.

Since she and Dale had resolved their concerns, Bev opened her mouth to refute the comment, but she saw her mother had more to say and quieted.

"So have we," Al said. "We thought maybe it's best to get all of this out in the open."

Bev felt her heart trip, wondering.

Al gestured toward her mother. "Millie and I have talked about our relationship for a long time. I think you both know that Dotty told me that Millie and I should get together after she was gone. I realize that sounds strange, but Dale can tell you his mother liked to be in charge." He gave Dale a tender grin.

Dale nodded. "That was Mom."

Al rose and crossed to Mildred's side. He rested his hands on the back of her chair. "We've made a decision, and we want you to know what it is."

Bev held her breath.

Her mother shifted forward and looked at Al over her shoulder. "Al and I have decided that what we need right now is to be best friends."

Bev felt the pent-up air leave her body. She glanced at Dale. He didn't bat an eye.

"Not that we haven't talked about possibilities," Al said, "but Millie and I aren't ready for anything yet."

"But that won't change the way we feel," Mildred said. "You can't beat a good friend, and we are open to God's leading."

Al shifted forward, sat on the arm of her mother's chair and grasped her hand. "One day, the future may hold surprises. Right, Millie?"

"Right," she said, smiling up at him.

Bev swallowed the lump in her throat. God was so good. When she put things in the Lord's hands, he made everything right, so unlike her own botched-up ways. Since she and Dale had opened their hearts, Bev prayed one day she and Dale could follow God's leading in the same kind of deep faith and trust.

"We're happy for you," Dale said, rising to kiss Millie's cheek.

Bev sat back, feeling the blessed assurance she'd prayed for for so long.

Dale didn't return to sit beside her, and Bev spotted an odd look on his face. It puzzled her. Before he could speak, Kristin bounded through the door, dragging in grass on her shoes and carrying a filled basket.

"Look what we found," she said, dumping the plastic eggs and green straw onto the carpet.

"Kristin," Bev said, amazed that she'd done that. Even more astounding, Michael came through the doorway in his stocking feet, set his basket on the carpet and plopped down beside it like a gentleman.

Disbelieving, Dale and Bev laughed at the hypothesis of what their future held.

"I'm ready for pie and coffee. Anyone else?" Dale asked.

"Sounds good to me," Al said, adjusting his tight belt buckle.

Millie chuckled and gave Al a poke. "I'll help," she said, standing.

"You sit," Dale said. "Bev and I'll get it."

"Look, Grandma," Kristin said. "I have a whole dollar."

"Speaking of dollars—" Al leaned over and dug into his back pants pocket "—I told you I'd…"

His voice faded as Bev reached the kitchen. She was surprised Dale had suggested dessert so quickly after dinner, but she was still learning about men's appetites.

When she turned, Dale stood behind her with the same strange look that had puzzled her. "Is something wrong?"

"Everything's right. Perfect, in fact." He drew her into his arms. "Isn't life wonderful when you let God be in charge?"

Bev tried to comment, but he interrupted her response.

"Somehow God in His wisdom brought two confused, hurting people together and created two complete people. You've made me the person I am, and I love you with all my heart."

Her mind swam with confusion. Could this be what it seemed?

"I realize that life is too lonely without you at my side. I've grown to love your kids. They make life even better." He clasped her hand, knelt beside her and kissed her fingers. "Bev, will you marry me?"

The words wrapped around her heart and caught in her throat. She struggled to answer without sobbing for joy. "You're everything I want, Dale. I would be proud and honored to be your wife."

He rose and pressed her against his chest as his lips found hers. The warmth traveled through her body while her pulse thundered. They'd lived so long on the edge the reality seemed impossible.

He deepened the kiss, and she tightened her arms around his neck. Her fingers caressed the nape of his neck, then found their way to his thick dark hair. She felt Dale's mouth move on hers, making her breathless. She'd so often questioned God's purpose, and today she heard His answer.

Dale shuddered and drew back. He looked at her through heavy-lidded eyes. "Love is the answer, Bev, and I promise with all my heart, I will never walk away. I will be by your side until God takes one of us home, and then one day we'll be together again. I promise."

"Grandpa wants to know where's the pie?"

Michael's voice burst into the room, and they jumped at the sound.

"Yuck," he said. "More kissing."

Before anything more was said, Michael vanished into the living room, his "yucks" echoing behind him. Bev heard her mother laugh and expected the whole family to come through the doorway, but no one did.

A broad grin lit Dale's face. "I suppose we have to live with these interruptions."

"I suppose," she said, still in his arms.

He paused a moment and studied her. "Do you think two kids are enough?"

His question snapped her to attention. "Enough for what?"

He chuckled. "Enough for a family. Would you consider one or two more?"

Bev searched his eyes for the joke. "You're kidding?"

"No, I'm not. I want to have another child or two. You'd make me the happiest man in the world."

Bev's arms entwined around his neck. "I'd have three more if you wanted them."

His look softened. "You'd do that for me?" he murmured.

"For us," she said.

He drew her closer as she rode on waves of happiness. His lips captured hers again, and she luxuriated in their warmth and tenderness. Dale Levin, a husband and father. God worked miracles, and today He'd truly worked one on them.

Dale brushed his nose against hers. "I suppose we should tell our folks."

She nodded, hating to move. "And the kids," she said.

"They already know."

Her heart stopped. "What?"

"I talked to them a few days ago on your birthday and got their permission. We've arranged everything to their liking."

"I can't believe it. They never said a word."

"Because it was our secret." He kissed the top of her head and urged her toward the living room.

"Finally," Al said, as they came through the doorway, but his expression changed as he eyed their empty hands. "Where's the dessert?"

"Bev and I have something to tell you."

Mildred gasped and brought her fist to her mouth.

"What's wrong, Mom?" Bev's pulse skittered at her mother's reaction.

"I hope this is what I've prayed for," Mildred said.

Tears bubbled in Bev's eyes, seeing her mother's joy.

Dale cleared his throat and wrapped his arm around Bev's shoulder. "I've asked Bev to be my wife, and she said yes."

"And we're going to be his kids," Michael said, his pitch rising with his excitement.

"We're going to get a new house," Kristin said.

Mildred's smile faded. "In Grand Rapids?"

"No, Grandma, right here in Loving."

"I'm so happy. Now that we've all been together in Loving, I'm spoiled."

"We've all been there," Dale said, giving Bev a knowing look with their private joke.

"You couldn't make us happier," Al said, reaching over and squeezing Mildred's hand.

Dale flexed his palm. "Before you all jump up with congratulations, I have something else to do." He bent down and pulled a plastic orb from beneath the chair. "I found another Easter egg, but this one's for Bev."

Bev looked at the bright-pink oval, and her heart stood still. She slid into the nearest chair and pulled the two sides of the egg apart with trembling hands. Inside, she found what she expected. A jeweler's ring box.

Kristin darted to her mother's side and hung over the chair arm.

Bev lifted the lid and gazed at the twinkling diamond set in yellow gold. The stone's fire took her breath away. "It's lovely, Dale."

"Not as lovely as you are."

He reached down, slid the ring from her hand, and slipped it onto her finger. Dale helped her rise, then kissed her tenderly before cuddling the children to them.

"Soon we'll be one happy family." He grinned. He reached over and gave Kristin's ponytail a playful yank. "What do you say, sweetie?"

She grabbed her hair and grinned. "I guess I have to get used to that. Right?"

"Want me to stop?" Dale asked.

Kristin shook her head. "Nope. I want you to love me just the way you do."

"I promise to love you all always."

Bev watched three adults wipe at their eyes just as she was doing. She looked at her children, seeing their joy and feeling complete for the first time.

"Thank you, Lord," she whispered, "for all Your loving promises."

* * * * *

*If you enjoyed LOVING PROMISES,
you'll love Gail's next inspirational romance,
LOVING FEELINGS,
available from Steeple Hill Love Inspired
in June 2005.*

Dear Reader,

Isn't God awesome? His timing is perfect. When we need Him, He's there, surrounding us with His love and mercy. I pray that you open your arms to the Lord when you have needs, as Bev and Dale did in *Loving Promises*. We all find times in our lives when problems press against us and hope seems to fade. This is the time we need to look away from our own ability and know that God is waiting for us to seek His help and give Him our burdens.

I hope you enjoyed another visit to Loving, Michigan. You met some new friends and visited with some townspeople you've come to know in previous stories. I'm pleased to let you know that you'll have more opportunities to visit with them again in *Loving Feelings*.

As always, I pray the Lord touches you with every blessing as you deal with life's ups and downs, and until we meet again, I wish you love and peace that only comes from He who gives us everything.

Gail Gaymer Martin

Send someone a little Inspiration this Easter with...

FTD.COM & *Love Inspired*

Purchase any 3 different Love Inspired titles in March 2005 and collect the coupon codes inside each book to **receive $10 off the purchase of flowers and gifts from FTD.COM!**

To take advantage of this offer, simply go to www.ftd.com/loveinspired and enter the coupon codes (in any order) from each of the 3 books! Or call 1-800-SEND-FTD and give promo code 10069.

Redeemable from March 1, 2005, to May 31, 2005. $10 discount applies to net purchase not including service, transaction, or shipping and handling fees and taxes. Offer valid to U.S. and Canadian residents only. Void where prohibited. Offer not valid in retail stores or in conjunction with any other offers from FTD.COM.

Happy Easter from Steeple Hill Books and FTD.COM!

Steeple Hill®

Don't forget— Mother's Day is just around the corner!

Take 2 inspirational love stories FREE!

PLUS get a FREE surprise gift!

Mail to Steeple Hill Reader Service™

In U.S.
3010 Walden Ave.
P.O. Box 1867
Buffalo, NY 14240-1867

In Canada
P.O. Box 609
Fort Erie, Ontario
L2A 5X3

YES! Please send me 2 free Love Inspired® novels and my free surprise gift. After receiving them, if I don't wish to receive anymore, I can return the shipping statement marked cancel. If I don't cancel, I will receive 4 brand-new novels every month, before they're available in stores! Bill me at the low price of $4.24 each in the U.S. and $4.74 each in Canada, plus 25¢ shipping and handling and applicable sales tax, if any*. That's the complete price and a savings of over 10% off the cover prices—quite a bargain! I understand that accepting the books and gift places me under no obligation ever to buy any books. I can always return a shipment and cancel at any time. Even if I never buy another book from Steeple Hill, the 2 free books and the surprise gift are mine to keep forever.

113 IDN DZ9M
313 IDN DZ9N

Name	(PLEASE PRINT)	
Address	Apt. No.	
City	State/Prov.	Zip/Postal Code

Not valid to current Love Inspired® subscribers.

Want to try two free books from another series?
Call 1-800-873-8635 or visit www.morefreebooks.com.

* Terms and prices are subject to change without notice. Sales tax applicable in New York. Canadian residents will be charged applicable provincial taxes and GST. All orders subject to approval. Offer limited to one per household.

® are registered trademarks owned and used by the trademark owner and or its licensee.

INTLI04R   ©2004 Steeple Hill